STO

FRIENDS
OF ACPL

ALLEN COUNTY PUBLIC LIBRARY

3 1833 00700 8672

W9-BYP-014

# Big Doin's
## ON RAZORBACK RIDGE

*Also by Ellis Credle*

Down, Down the Mountain
Big Fraid, Little Fraid
Tall Tales from the High Hills

# Big Doin's
## ON RAZORBACK RIDGE

WRITTEN AND ILLUSTRATED BY

## Ellis Credle

THOMAS NELSON INC., PUBLISHERS

Nashville          New York

No character in this book is intended to represent any actual person; all the incidents of the story are entirely fictional in nature.

Copyright © 1956 by Ellis Credle

All rights reserved under International and Pan-American Conventions. Published in Nashville, Tennessee, by Thomas Nelson Inc., Publishers, and simultaneously in Don Mills, Ontario, by Thomas Nelson & Sons (Canada) Limited. Manufactured in the United States of America.

*This edition published March 1978*

Library of Congress Cataloging in Publication Data

Credle, Ellis.
  Big doin's on Razorback Ridge

  SUMMARY: The President is coming to the opening of the new dam, and the mountain people of Razorback Ridge are excited, especially Jody and Nancy, who are determined to win the prize for the best entertainment.
  [1. Mountain life—fiction.]   I. Title
PZ7.C861Bi  1978  [Fic]  77-27803
ISBN 0-8407-6607-6

*To My Friends in Beaverdam Valley*

CO. SCHOOLS
C863970

# Contents

The Honey Hunt . . . . . . . . . . . . .  9

Buggy with the Boogie . . . . . . . . . .  34

Traipsing Round the Mountain . . . . . . .  49

The Delectable Mountains . . . . . . . . .  83

Right Outen the Sky . . . . . . . . . . . 102

# 1. The Honey Hunt

Nancy Calloway leaned over the curb and peered into the well. Far down she could see her own reflection—a round, freckled face with lively blue eyes and hair the color of winter broom sage. Then she let the wooden bucket run with full force through the pulley. It hit the water with an angry splash.

"There!" That splash always made her feel better. It was the only way she could express her feelings about drawing water without being mean and selfish. Every day eight buckets had to be pulled up, and even more on washday. It was heavy, weary work. But who else was there to do it now? Pappy was hard put to get his corn cultivated and had no time for it. Her brother Zach was away working on the dam the government was a-building across Little Turkey River, and Fern, her sister, was in Mountain City most of the time going to high school. Mammy didn't even try to draw water any more. She was plumb worn out with it. Nancy hauled and hauled away. She was on the sixth bucket when she paused, listening. Had someone called her name?

It came again, small with the distance: "Nance-e-e!"

Nancy set the bucket on the well-curb and gazed off over the valley. It was just after sunup and the mountains looked pale and wan. Mist was rising like smoke from all the hollows. But over on the shaggy sides of Old Smoky, across the way, she could make out a small clearing with a cabin of squared-off logs. In front of it was a thin figure in faded blue jeans—her Cousin Jodey. It was a long way to Jodey's house, a good hour's journey if you walked it. But across the valley, as the crow flew, it was close enough for shouting.

"Nance-e-e!" Jodey waved a feed-basket to catch her eye.

Nancy took a long breath. Her words went winging out: "Hi, Jodey!"

In a moment Jodey's voice came again: "Uncle Badger's going hunting a wild beehive today. Want to go?"

"Sure do! Wait a minute, I'll ask Mammy."

"Ask Dora, too," Jodey's voice came over. "Uncle Badger needs help. Says he's got to find a real humdinger this time. Going to make a whole barrel full of pink lemonade. Needs a lot of sweetening."

"What say—a whole barrel full?" Nancy wasn't sure she had heard aright.

"Sure as shooting. Maybe two barrels full. Going to be some big doin's here on Razorback Ridge."

"Doin's—what for?"

"Just take a guess."

Nancy pondered. "Granny Gruber's old piedy cow has borned another two-headed calf. They're a-going to charge to see it and sell lemonade!"

"No!"

"There's a-going to be another turkey shoot."

"No, nothing like that."

"Tell me." Nancy yelled. "I give up."

"The big government dam across Little Turkey River is all finished. The President is a-coming to speechify!"

"The President of the whole United States?" Nancy shouted.

"Yep!" Jodey's voice floated over. "The fellows that work on the dam want us to put on a big dance contest for the doin's. They've raised the money for two big prizes, one for the lady and one for the gent!"

"Whoopee!" Nancy's heart gave a bounce. She broke into a lively jig. Dancing was her hobby—a hobby shared by Jodey. "What's the prize?" she called.

"They're not a-telling. It's a secret!"

"Gollies! Wouldn't it be nice to get that prize!"

Across the mist of the valley, Nancy could see Jodey cutting a merry shuffle. "It's as good as in the bag!" his cocksure words came across.

Nancy laughed. "I'll go ask Mammy and see if Dora can go."

As Nancy turned and bounded up the back steps she thought about their dances. She and Jodey had always had a hankering for the old-time steps, the clogs and jigs and flings that had come over the ocean with the earliest settlers. They had traipsed the mountains together, searching out the old folks who could teach them. And they had practiced by the hour. Sometimes at the square dances, when the grownups were resting between sets, people shouted for Jodey and Nancy to dance. It was fun to get out on the floor and fling into an old-time jig. And everybody was always pleased a sight.

"Don't you forget them old steps," Granny Gruber had said to Nancy. "Each one is a keepsake from the past. Folks up here in the mountains are forgetting the old days and the old ways. If somebody don't remember 'em and pass 'em down to the next set of young'uns, they'll soon be forgot and lost. Child, hit's a great thing you and Jodey have learned 'em."

How wonderful if they would be called on to dance at the big doin's for the dam! What a fine chance to show off the old-time steps so they'd not be forgotten!

Nancy whisked through the door to ask her mother about the honey hunt. When Mammy heard about the doin's she was almost as excited as Nancy. She began to fly around with her housecleaning as if getting ready for it right that moment.

"The President a-coming, land sakes!" she cried. "We'd ought to get together and make him a nice present—a keepsake of his trip to the mountains! What did you say? Jodey wants you to go on a honey hunt? Why yes, run along." Then her voice became stern. "But you watch now and don't let that Jodey lead you and Dora into mischief out there in the hills!"

"Why no, Mammy. What sort of mischief could he get us into?"

"There's no telling, no telling at all what that boy will think up. He's a rascal."

"I'll be careful, Mammy!" Nancy promised as she ran out again to call Dora, her best friend, who lived in a little cabin across the hollow.

Dora jumped with delight to hear of the honey hunt and promised to be ready in a few minutes.

Nancy went back to report to Jodey. "We can go!" she shouted across the stretch of blue air.

Jodey waved the feed-basket. "Meet you at the crossroads in half an hour!"

Nancy quickly hauled up the last two buckets of water, lugged them into the kitchen, and poured them into the tub on the kitchen table.

Mammy looked up from her dishwashing. "Better take along something to eat," she advised. "Old Badger never knows when to come home. He forgets all about the time. Like as not you'll be out all day. But he *is* a great one for finding honey. Another fellow can go out and comb the mountains and come home empty-handed, and Badger can follow right in his tracks and find a barrel of honey. How he does it, I don't know. He must have a method. Or else—" Mammy looked cautiously over her shoulder and lowered her voice, "he's a witchman and does it by magic. That's what *some* folks say."

Nancy looked startled. Uncle Badger a witchman? The thought made her feel shivery. As she went to the tin safe for some fried ham to make sandwiches, she silently made up her mind to watch and try to spy out Uncle Badger's secret if she could. Would he cast a spell? she asked herself. And how did witches cast spells? A small tingle of fear went down her spine as she tried to remember all she had heard about witches. They could blacken their arms to the elbows with soot, clap their hands, and fly right up the chimney. They could jump right out of their skins and then they could take the shapes of cats or dogs

or bats or whatever they wanted to. They could take the parings of a body's fingernails, tie them into a bundle with things like feathers or snakeskins, and bury them under the doorstep. Then they'd have power to make that person do what they wanted.

"What are you going to do with all that ham and biscuit?" Nancy's sister, Fern, came into the kitchen and began to skim the cream from the milk.

"Going off with Uncle Badger to hunt a wild beehive."

"Uncle Badger! Listen, Nancy, you ought not to hang around Uncle Badger so much."

"Why not?" Nancy split open the biscuits and laid a slice of ham in each one.

"He's ignorant. He doesn't know how to read—can't even write his own name. Why, he doesn't even live in a house like other people. A cave in the mountains. That's the way animals live—wildcats and bears and things."

"I don't care. I don't care if he does live in a cave. I don't care if he can't write his name. He knows lots of things, lots and lots of things that other people don't know!" Nancy found a tin bucket for bringing home the honey. "You come with us, Fern, you'll see. It's fun out on the mountains and you can learn a lot from Uncle Badger, honest you can."

"I'd rather go to the movies in Mountain City." Fern poured the cream into the churn, sat down before it, and began to thump the dasher up and down to make the butter come. "I have a lot more fun there and learn a lot more, too. I just hope I can get me a job after I get through the Mountain City High School. I'll have some pretty clothes and some modernistic furniture with satin coverlets like they do in the movies. None of these old-timy spool beds and pieced quilts for me!"

Nancy looked at her sister in shocked surprise. What could be prettier than Mammy's pieced quilts? But there was no time to argue with her now.

"Good-by, Mammy." She kissed her mother's cheek and ran out the door.

On the road, she followed the zigzag rail fence that enclosed her pappy's cornfield. She waved to Pappy who was out there hoeing.

"Where you off to?" he called out.

"Going hunting a wild beehive with Uncle Badger."

"Bring me home a bucket of honey! Anybody working in a field like this needs something to sweeten his disposition. It's the porest piece of land in the Blue Ridge Mountains. Even the rabbits know it."

Nancy paused. "The rabbits, Pappy?"

"Why sure. A little while ago what did I see but a little old bunny running along a furrow with a paper sack in his paw. I asked him what he had there and he said it was a little snack. When he had to cross this field, he said, he needed something to keep from starving before he got to the other side."

Nancy laughed, though she felt uneasy too. Although Pappy laughed and made jokes about his land, they all knew it was no joking matter. The rains rushing down the mountainsides were washing away all their good topsoil. The corn turned out scrawnier and scrawnier each season, and they were getting poorer every year. No chance of a new dress for the doin's. Nancy sighed and hurried on.

At the little cottage where Dora lived with her great-aunt, Miss Lizzie Sprockett, Nancy called out and her friend came running, her tight pigtails flying out behind. The two girls hurried along the road which ran along the edge of the mountain.

"We'd better look out for Aunt Rhoda's old spotted sow," Nancy said as they came abreast of a small cabin set back among clumps of pink mountain laurel. "There's not a meaner-natured old beast on Razorback Ridge. The old critter is always running out and attacking people. I think she just enjoys seeing 'em jump fences and climb trees."

"There she is now," said Dora, "outen her pen!"

The two girls cast frightened glances toward the sow, but she was busy chewing away on acorns beneath a scrawny oak tree and didn't look up. They hurried on and breathed sighs of relief when they were well past the house. In a steep cornfield a little beyond, Aunt Rhoda and Uncle Joe were busy hoeing corn. Their little daughter, Rowena, was hoeing along with them.

"Hey there, you'uns!" Nancy and Dora called out.

"Hey there, yourselves!" those in the field replied.

"Aren't you afraid you'll fall outen that field and break your necks?" Nancy called out.

The three in the cornfield laughed. It was an old mountain joke. But not a very funny one, they thought, if a body peered over the edge to the valley down below.

"This here is the kind of field the old folks used to plant with a shotgun," Uncle Joe said. "They'd load up with corn, stand off, and bang away at it. That's all there was to planting in the old days and the ground was so rich the corn would spring up high as a house without even hoeing it."

"Golly, that was nice!" Nancy exclaimed. Then she asked, "Couldn't Rowena go with us to hunt a beehive?"

"I reckon not today," said Aunt Rhoda. "This old field isn't what it used to be. It's so worn out now it takes the whole family working at it to coax up enough corn to make our corn pone for the winter."

The girls walked on. Suddenly they stopped, alarmed. Dirt and stones were rattling down the hillside. A landslide! The whole mountainside might be coming down—it might bury them! They clasped each other in terror. Then, of a sudden, Jodey appeared sliding down the hill on the seat of his jeans.

"Landsakes, you scared us near 'bout to death, we thought you were a landslide!" Nancy cried.

"You'll wear holes in your pants that-a-way!" Dora exclaimed.

"The other way—walking round the mountain with one foot on the high side and t'other one on the low side, I'll get like a sidehill gouger," Jodey retorted.

"Sidehill gouger—what's that?" Dora asked.

"Oh, you know that funny animal Uncle Badger talks about.

He walks around the mountain so much with one leg on the high side and t'other one on the low side that he gets lop-sided. His legs on one side are long and the ones on the other side are short."

"Oh, shucks," laughed the girls. "You know Uncle Badger's just a-joking. There's no such animal." The three walked on together. Rounding a bend they came upon Uncle Badger seated on a rock, his gun across his lap and his hunting dog, old Major, beside him. He was a lean old man in faded clothes and shoes he had made himself from raw cowhide.

"Hey there, young'uns!" Uncle Badger called out. "Good thing you've got those buckets. People that don't bring buckets don't go honey-hunting with me!"

"No?" The children look at him inquiringly.

"No sir! Going hunting for a beehive without a bucket is as bad as going to church to pray for rain without an umbrella. You've got to expect what you go after or you don't get it."

"I see," Nancy said. The others nodded thoughtfully.

"Well, all here now? Let's get going." Uncle Badger stood up and shouldered his gun. "We've got to get the sweetening for that pink lemonade. Going to have barrels full, I reckon. Nancy, go round by that big rock where that honeysuckle is a-blooming. Break off some sprigs. Bring a whole bouquet."

"What fur?" Nancy's voice was puzzled.

"What fur? Cat's fur. To make kittens' britches!" Uncle Badger replied and would make no further explanation.

Nancy got the honeysuckle, wondering as she plucked it, if it had something to do with Uncle Badger's magic for finding honey.

The little party, led by Major, climbed a gentle slope where the pine trees made a soft whirring sound, and their feet slid on the slippery carpet of needles.

"I guess we'd better look into all the trees," Jodey suggested to Uncle Badger. "Especially the ones that might have a hollow where the bees could make a hive."

"No need of that, no need," Uncle Badger discouraged him. "That's no way to find a beehive. There's millions of trees in the woods. You can't go looking into every one."

Dora looked at Nancy in perplexity. If Uncle Badger didn't look into the trees, how did he find the hives?

"Folks say he's a witchman and finds the beehives by magic," Nancy whispered.

"Land sakes!" Dora's eyes grew as round as saucers.

They climbed from the pine woods up a steep, rocky incline, pulling themselves up by the sassafras bushes, finding footing on the flat ledges. It was hard climbing. When at last they reached the top they rested, hot and panting, on a high plain swept by a cool mountain wind. The children stood ankle-deep in wild strawberries. Overhead two crows went cawing in the vast blue sky.

"My, but this is fine!" Nancy turned her warm little face into the breeze.

"This is better still!" Jodey crammed his mouth full of strawberries.

Major began to tear around in circles, bewitched by the sunshine, the smell of wild strawberries, and the joy of being there with Uncle Badger and the children. Laughing, they watched his crazy circlings.

Dora peered over the edge of the mountain. "Looky, we've

climbed away up higher than the tops of the pine trees. You could jump right over 'em if you gave a good spring."

"You'd land pretty hard if you did!" Jodey said.

"Looky, 'way over yonder," Nancy said, pointing, "there's the big government dam where Zach's a-working."

"Whooey! It's made a monster-sized lake outen Little Turkey River, hasn't it?" Dora said.

"I don't even want to see it." Uncle Badger turned away. "My boyhood home is away down there under twenty feet of water. Near about killed me when the government moved me outen there and onto another place. I don't think the government's got any business flooding folks' farms and a-changing the land from the way God made it."

"Zach says the dam is going to make things a lot better for us up here in the hills." Nancy looked at Uncle Badger uncertainly. "He says it's a-going to make electricity and we'll have electric lights and electric iceboxes where victuals keep just like in the wintertime."

"Shucks, honey, that's all humbug talk. Them boxes cost a mountain of money—more money than most of us up here have seen at one time in our whole lives. How could we'uns ever buy things like that?"

"I reckon that dam is for folks from beyond," said Dora wistfully.

"It ain't for pore mountain folks like us, and that's certain," said Uncle Badger.

"Look at those little bitty houses down there." Nancy pointed toward two mossy roofs far below. "Why, it's Mr. MacMurray's mill and Bluett MacMurray's house right beside it. I never recognized 'em from up here on top."

"I bet I could throw a rock right down into the chimney," Jodey said. He picked up a round stone and threw it out into space.

The girls watched it fall. It rattled down upon the roof of the house below.

"This'll go better—just watch!" He let fly another as large as a baseball. Down . . . down . . . down . . .

The girls let out a shriek as it fell exactly into the chimney.

Almost instantly a little girl ran out of the door down below. She looked up at the chimney, then catching sight of the children on the mountain above, she shouted: "You, Jodey, I know that was you! What did you throw into our chimney? It fell right into the pot of turnip greens cooking on the hearth."

"Just tossed in a dumpling for you, Bluett," Jodey shouted back.

They all laughed, Bluett with them.

"Let's go on now, young'uns. No beehives around here," Uncle Badger said.

Following his long strides, the children trotted across the high plateau and entered the woods that grew upon the mountainsides beyond. It was dim and cool among the towering trunks. Major, sniffing importantly, went ranging ahead. When at last they came upon a small stream gurgling busily over the rocks, they shouted with delight and sat down to shuck off shoes and stockings. Even Uncle Badger took off his brogans and began to wade. How cool the water was, rippling over their bare feet! Major went wading too, splashing foolishly now and then as he tried to pounce on some darting water insect.

They waded along through the shallow bubbling water, spotted with sunlight falling through the branches. When they came to an open glade, Uncle Badger paused and looked about.

"Get your shoes on, young'uns," he ordered. "This is where we'll get on the track of them bees."

The children looked around mystified. What was there here to make Uncle Badger say it was a good place to find bees? But they came out of the water and did as he said. They were still more puzzled when he took a hatchet from his belt and began to chop down a tall, slender sapling. After it was down he unfastened a leather case from his belt and tossed it to Jodey.

"You can trim off the branches while I do some digging."

Things were getting more and more mysterious.

Jodey drew a hunting knife from the case while Uncle Badger walked out into the meadow, away from the trees, and began to dig a hole with his hatchet.

Was Uncle Badger making a magic spell? Nancy was too full of curiosity to contain herself. "What's that fur?" she asked.

"Cat's fur, to make kittens' britches!" was Uncle Badger's only explanation.

Jodey soon had the tree trimmed of all its branches. Uncle Badger took it, and made a small slit at the very top.

"Now!" he said to Nancy in a tone of satisfaction. "Hand me a sprig of that there honeysuckle!"

Nancy nodded knowingly at Dora as she picked out a sprig. What was Uncle Badger doing if not making magic? They stared at the old man as he fastened the honeysuckle in the split he had just made and walked out into the meadow and planted the sapling in the hole. There it stood, upright, with the honeysuckle shining in the sun high up in the air.

Nancy and Dora peered up at it with popping eyes. Yes sir, as sure as shooting, Uncle Badger was making witchcraft!

But then the old man began to explain. "An old Cherokee Indian taught me that trick long ago when I was a young'un," he said with pride. The children looked at each other blankly.

Then Jodey's face lit up. "Oh, I catch on. The honeysuckle draws the bees—is that it?"

"That's right. If there's a bee anywhere for miles around he'll scent that honeysuckle. He'll come a-winging. He'll crawl into one of them pretties, load up with nectar, and then he'll make a beeline for home."

"What do we do then, Uncle Badger?" Jodey asked.

"We follow him, young'un, just as fast as we can gallop."

"But how can we see a little bitty thing like a bee flying up among the branches of the trees?" Dora exclaimed. "Seems like we'd lose it in no time."

Uncle Badger patted his breast pocket and winked knowingly. "I've got some magic here."

Magic—so it was true after all! Nancy's heart gave a bump.

The children craned their necks as he took out a worn leather case. "Got these at the ten-cent store." He slipped a pair of spectacles from the case and opened them. "Put 'em on, Nancy, and look at old Major there."

Nancy put on the spectacles. "Whillikers! Why—why—old Major looks as big as a cow!"

"Let me look!"

"Me!"

The others must try the spectacles. Through their magnifying lenses grasshoppers became fearsome creatures and small darting lizards were transformed into baby dragons.

"You see, young'uns, with these here, a bee looks as big as a buzzard. You can run after him as long as you can keep up.

When you're all tuckered out, you can set up another pole and wait for another bee."

Nancy gave Dora a look. No witchcraft about it. It was just that Uncle Badger always found out ways to do things that other people didn't think of. They gazed at him admiringly.

For a long time they sat waiting for bees to appear. "Maybe we could eat our vittles while we watch," Dora said.

The suggestion met with enthusiastic approval and soon a picnic lunch was spread out on a smooth white boulder at the edge of the water. They all set to, hungrily.

"Wonder what the prizes for the dance contest are going to be?" remarked Dora, biting first into a chicken leg, then into a buttered biscuit.

"Hit's a secret, they say." Uncle Badger unrolled a juicy baked yam from a piece of newspaper. "But one of the boys from the dam gave me a little hint. They've made up a jingle about it." He quoted:

> Not much bigger than a pumpkin-head,
> Heavy as lead and colored red.
> It will pleasure young or old,
> Man or woman, I am told.

"Land sakes, whatever can that be?" Nancy chewed thoughtfully on a mouthful of fried ham and biscuit.

All during the meal the young folks kept trying to guess the meaning of the verse. "Something that pleases man or woman, young or old." Jodey was puzzled. "Now what could it be?" He bit thoughtfully into the slice of scrapple he held in one hand, then into the piece of cornbread in the other hand. Suddenly he looked up. "I know. It's a cherry pie!"

"A cherry pie?"

"But that's not heavy as lead. Leastways, it ought not to be," Dora said. "It's not much of a pie if it's heavy as lead."

"If it's chock-a-block full of cherries, maybe it's heavy as lead," Jodey contended. "I'll bet you a pretty that's just what it is." Then he burst out, pointing, "Looky, there goes a bee into the honeysuckle!"

Uncle Badger hurriedly put on his spectacles and snatched up his gun. "Come on, young'uns, be prepared for a run!"

The bee crept purposefully into one of the blossoms. It crawled out again, wiggled its feelers and took off.

Off dashed Uncle Badger, the children at his heels. Bushes slapped them and brambles caught at them, but they rushed on. When at last they felt they could not take another breath, Uncle Badger slowed down and stood gasping.

"I'm clean tuckered out. We'll rest a spell."

They sat down, Major with them, panting. After a while they got up and set up another pole with the bee bait. This time five or six bees appeared almost instantly. Uncle Badger exclaimed triumphantly that they must be near the hive.

The small cluster of bees flew off and led their pursuers straight to an ancient gum tree that was broken off at the top. High up from the ground a large hollow could be seen where bees were busily flying in and out.

"There 'tis," shouted Uncle Badger, waving his gun.

"There 'tis, whoopee!" yelled the children. Major capered about, barking as proudly as if he, himself, had led them to the find.

"Look, two hollows!" Uncle Badger was jubilant. "No bees

going in or out the one up above. I'll bet they sealed off enough honey up there to last a lifetime!"

"But look, Uncle Badger, how high up!" Jodey said. "How will we ever get up there to get it out?"

They circled the tree, perplexed. The trunk was immense. No pair of arms could reach around it and it rose straight up without a limb, high into the air.

"I declare, it's nigh got me buffaloed," Uncle Badger wrinkled his brow in thought. "And there's another problem, too—how to steal the honey without stirring up the bees. Barging right into a beehive is worse than slapping a wildcat in the face. A body can get stung clean to death that way."

Out in the bushes, old Major suddenly began to yelp excitedly, as though he had unexpectedly run onto some animal. Then they could hear him running off into the woods, barking his head off.

Uncle Badger quickly turned his head. "What's he raised, now, I wonder?"

"A rabbit, maybe," suggested Nancy.

"Something bigger'n a rabbit!" Jodey exclaimed. "A good hunting dog's got a different kind of bark for different animals. That's no rabbit bark!"

"A bear, maybe, or a wildcat!" Uncle Badger was full of excitement. "Stay here, young'uns, I'm going to see what 'tis!" He dashed away. In a moment he was lost to sight among the trees.

The children stood looking at each other, bewildered at being left so suddenly. Then, as Major's barking became fainter with the distance, they turned back to the bee tree.

"You see this tall tree right next to it," Jodey said. "One of its limbs leans right over that old broken top. I could shinny up it and look right over into it." He slapped the smaller tree thoughtfully.

"You'd better not," Dora warned. "You know what Uncle Badger said about the bees stinging."

"Shucks, there aren't any bees 'way up there. You heard Uncle Badger say it was sealed off." Jodey began to kick off his shoes.

The girls watched, a little worried, as he shinnied up the tree. He began to shunt himself along the limb that leaned over the broken bee tree.

"Gee whiz, this is queer!" he paused and examined the limb. "This limb is as smooth as glass. It looks like somebody's shunted along here lots of times before."

"It's just weathered, maybe," Dora said.

"Maybe—" Jodey looked doubtful. He inched along until he was just above the bee tree. The limb bent a little with his weight. "Why, I could climb right down into the hollow. Look, my feet touch!"

"Don't you do it. You might get stung!" The girls were alarmed.

"I can see some honeycombs in there. Yummy! I'll cut some out with Uncle Badger's knife—" Jodey began to let himself carefully into the hollow.

"Wait, Jodey, wait for Uncle Badger!" came frightened warnings from below.

Jodey ignored them and disappeared into the top of the tree.

Dora and Nancy looked at each other. "Suppose he cuts right down to where the bees are!"

"We'd better holler for Uncle Badger."

"Don't holler here. We might stir up the bees. Get off a little."

They rushed off into the bushes and began to shout: "Uncle Badger, come back! Uncle Badger!"

Came a hail from not far away: "I'm a-coming!"

The girls ran back to the tree. Arriving in the clearing, a sight met their eyes that froze them with horror. There was not a sign of Jodey, but shunting himself backward along the limb of the tall tree was a shaggy black beast.

"A bear!" The girls tumbled back into the bushes. They peered out to see the animal swinging himself into the hollow of the honey tree.

"Jodey!" screamed Nancy. "A bear! He's going down in the hollow!"

For a moment there was no sound. Then Jodey's voice came through the opening. "Oh, quit your kidding—you can't scare me. There's lots of honey in here. I'm a-cutting out some combs. Watch now and hold your buckets under this hole."

They saw Jodey's hand, holding a dripping honeycomb, emerge from a hole in the side of the tree. "Ready with the buckets now, I'm—"

Then to their horror his voice broke into a sudden squeal. The heavy comb fell with a squash. There was a terrifying roar from the bear, sounds of a struggle inside the trunk. Dora and Nancy clasped each other in terror. Frightful roars were sounding inside the hollow tree. Then, unexpectedly, the bear's black head popped from the top of the tree. His little beady eyes looked wild and frightened. His two great paws grasped the overhanging limb. He swung himself out of the hollow. In frantic haste he began to shunt himself along the limb.

A gun suddenly thundered. The girls clapped their hands to their ears. Uncle Badger appeared from the bushes, his gun smoking.

"Missed him, by gum!" he exclaimed as the bear went humping away through the bushes.

Major ran barking after him. But Uncle Badger called him back. "We haven't got time now to go off chasing a bear. It's getting late." He turned to the girls. "I reckon that old bear is what he got a scent of just now." Then he noticed their frightened faces. "What happened here? Where's Jodey?" he exclaimed in alarm.

The girls could hardly answer for terror. Was Jodey alive? What had happened up there inside the tree? While they were stammering, Jodey's head emerged out of the hollow. His hair was rumpled, his eyes popping.

"It *was* a bear!" he managed to gasp. "I thought you girls were joking when you said it was a bear. I thought you'd made it up just to scare me."

"What—what happened? Are you hurt? What made the bear jump out in such a hurry?" Uncle Badger and the girls asked questions all at once.

"I don't rightly know." Jodey scratched his hair into wilder disorder. "It got dark in there all of a sudden. I thought maybe it was Uncle Badger climbing in. But then I smelled that strong animal smell. I saw a hairy black leg coming down beside my face—the claws stuck into the side of the tree. Then I knew it *was* a bear. Lucky I had Uncle Badger's knife. I just reached up and gave that critter a jab in the behind. He went outen there in a hurry!"

Uncle Badger and the girls laughed in delighted admiration.

"Boy, you sure startled that old bruin!" Uncle Badger said. "He came outen that tree like he was shot outen a gun. You're a bear-fighter and no mistake. Old Dan'l Boone must of been your granddaddy."

Jodey laughed.

"Well, son, now you're up there, cut us out some honeycombs. But hurry—it looks like these bees are getting a mite nervous."

Jodey disappeared again and dripping combs began to plop, one by one, from the hole in the side of the tree. They were neatly caught by the buckets which Uncle Badger held underneath.

"One thing sure, there won't be any lack of sweetening for the big doin's," Uncle Badger said as they started the long trek home.

Nancy and Jodey and Dora nodded their heads with satisfaction. It had been a profitable day—and an exciting one!

## 2. Buggy with the Boogie

News of the big doin's at the dam went flying through the rugged mountain land. It was whooped across valleys and shouted across hollows. People flapped aprons at kinfolk on the other side of scrawny cornfields, they blew cowhorns to call neighbors on opposite mountains. By the time Uncle Badger and the children reached home, the word had spread to the lonesomest cabins on the farthest ranges. It had been decided that a meeting to plan the affair should be held in the schoolhouse Saturday.

On the afternoon of the meeting Pappy Calloway hitched the horse to the jolt-wagon and he and Mammy and Nancy and Fern all rode down the mountain together. It was unusually chilly for an early June day, a cold wind was blustering through the valley. Clouds were blowing across the sky, streaming raggedly between the high peaks of Old Smoky. But Nancy scarcely felt the cold. She was thinking of their dances. Which would be better for the doin's? The Irish jig was loud and lively, with the dancers' feet clacking like mad. People always clapped for that fit to bring the house down. The Scotch fling was nimble and gay the way she and Jodey did it, flinging their hands over their heads while their feet pranced on with the music. There was the hornpipe which everybody liked. And then there was the orangutang that fairly put them out of breath it was so fast, and that German dance that Granny Gruber had taught them. That was a good one, too, with lots of whirling and turning that made her skirts fly out like an umbrella. Oh, they were all so merry and each one so different it was hard to decide. She'd talk it over with Jodey and see which one he liked best.

Then another thought struck Nancy. Suppose the grown folks overlooked them when they made plans for the affair. Suppose they forgot them altogether. At the square dances it happened sometimes. The grown folks got so wound up in their own dancing and got to having such a good time they clean forgot Jodey and Nancy. Oh, it would never do to let that happen. She and Jodey just had to be in that dance contest! C863970 CO. SCHOOLS

Would it be all right, Nancy asked herself, to get up in the meeting and say right out that she and Jodey wanted to do one of their dances at the affair? No, that wouldn't do. It would be too forward. Maybe she could make a little speech and explain that the old dances were keepsakes from the past, as Granny Gruber had told her, and shouldn't be forgotten. But if she did, maybe they wouldn't listen. Or maybe they'd just think she was silly, they'd laugh and tell her to sit down—that children should be seen and not heard. Nancy felt worried and uncertain. She would look for Jodey as soon as she got there, she decided. Maybe he would know what to do.

What a crowd there was in the schoolyard when they arrived! Nancy waved at Bluett who was climbing out of the MacMurray's jalopy that was still puffing from its climb over the ridges. She spied Jodey seated with his parents in a wagon drawn by their old gray horse. She jumped out of the jolt-wagon and ran over to him, passing among saddle horses and mules and buggies that were tied to low-hanging limbs or drawn up at the rail fence that enclosed the yard.

She said "howdy" to Jodey and his family and stood waiting while they got out of the cart and fastened the horse. Then she drew Jodey aside and told him what was on her mind.

"Gee whillikers, I haven't got any more notion what to do than you have," Jodey said. He rubbed his hair into wild disorder. "Maybe we ought to just go in and listen and see what happens. Then maybe we'll know what to do."

They climbed the schoolhouse steps together.

"Hey there, young'uns!" said a voice behind them.

They looked around. Great-uncle Rufus was there, mounting the steps, his little niece, Ella, hanging onto one arm, his fiddle under the other. "I hear tell you had a little set-to with a bear," Uncle Rufus grinned at Jodey.

"Kind of," Jodey admitted, grinning back at him.

"Young'un, you should of hung onto that bear's tail when he hove outen that hole. Just look at your hair sticking six ways for Sunday! You can't go to no celebration looking like that. You need some slicking up with bear grease. That old bruin would have made you a tubful."

Jodey began to smooth his cowlicked hair.

"Shucks, Uncle Rufus," Ella said scornfully, "you don't have to go out and kill a bear nowadays to get your hair-stickum. You can go to town and buy a bottle in the ten-cent store."

"Huh! Me and Jodey, we'd ruther get into an old hollow tree and wrastle an old bruin hand-to-hand for our grease, hadn't we, son?"

"A sight ruther," Jodey agreed.

Inside the little schoolhouse people were packed from wall to wall. It was quite warm. A fire had been built in the small iron stove and the air was heated further with arguments. Everybody was having his say. They all felt free to do so because the Ridge community was one big family. Uncle Badger often said that if a body began to trace his kinship in the Blue Ridge Mountains, he'd soon find out he was his own grandmother. And now all these kinfolk were beginning to disagree.

"We haven't got time to weave any coverlet for the President," Granny Gruber was saying tartly as Nancy and Jodey entered. She shook her finger at Aunt Rhoda. "There's ne'er a bit of use to get started on something we can't finish!"

"Now, now, folks, don't get het up." Grandpa Gruber, who was sitting on the platform acting as chairman, smoothed his white corn-silk beard. "Maybe we could think of some other present for the President. Something that wouldn't take so long to make. Any suggestions?"

"I say make him a patchwork quilt," Nancy's mammy spoke up.

The word "patchwork" made Nancy's heart sink. The very sound of it gave her the jimmies.

"Don't it take even longer to patch a quilt?" demanded Aunt Rhoda.

"We can all work on a quilt at once," Mammy replied. "Even the young'uns can cut and sew quilt squares. But weaving a coverlet is a different matter. There's room for only one person at the loom, so only one at a time can work on it."

How awful if she were set to sewing quilt squares, Nancy thought. How could she and Jodey ever find time to practice their dances if she had to sit stitching all day long? And they did need to practice if they were to dance at the big doin's. They hadn't worked together in a coon's age.

"We could all meet at our house tomorrow afternoon," Mammy went on, "decide on the pattern, and get the whole thing cut out. We could take the squares home with us, sew all we could ourselves and put the young'uns to work on the rest. That way, all working together, we could have a quilt done in a few days."

The women all nodded agreement. "Yes, it could be done."

Nancy glanced around the room to see how her friends were taking this. Dora's round little face was puckered into an unhappy frown. Bluett MacMurray and Rowena looked as glum as owls, and Ella, sitting beside Uncle Rufus, was gazing up at the ceiling as if she wished something would fall and scatter all thoughts of a patchwork quilt.

"I say let's buy him something up-to-date," Fern called out. "Why not all club in together and buy him a satin quilt like the ones you see in the movies?"

Nancy and her friends suddenly brightened. Maybe this suggestion would save them.

"A satin quilt—who's got money to buy a satin quilt!" their

mammies overruled Fern's idea indignantly. "Even if we all pitched in, we'd not be able to buy a thing like that."

"Well, ladies, what say we take a vote?" Grandpa Gruber suggested. "All in favor of making a patchwork quilt for the President, hold up your hands." He nodded as hands went up all over the room, then carefully counted them. "Well," he said at length, "a patchwork quilt it's to be."

"Then all meet tomorrow afternoon at my house," Nancy's mammy called out. "And don't forget to bring the young'uns!"

The little girls looked at each other and groaned. A plague on the big doin's if they had to sit and sew quilt scraps from now till then!

"Now that's attended to we'll go on to the next question," said Grandpa Gruber. "Uncle Badger and the young'uns there—" he motioned toward Jodey and Nancy and Dora, "have already got the sweetening for some pink lemonade. So no need to worry over refreshments. And the boys at the dam have raised money for prizes for a dance contest. So that's settled, too. Now, what with the President's speech, do you folks think we need any other kind of entertainment?"

"We could have a turkey shoot," Uncle Badger shouted from the back of the room. "We could show the President some fancy shooting."

"A cornhusking," someone called out.

"Why no," someone else objected. "Seeing a bunch of fellows just sitting shucking corn to see which one can shuck the fastest ain't a-going to pleasure the President."

"I think some old ballads would be nice," Granny Gruber spoke up. "Let Aunt Rhoda there bring her dulcimer and sing the ballad of *The Frozen Girl, Sweet Barbara Allen,* or some of the others. To my mind, there's nothing purtier than the old ballads."

"Oh, Granny, those old songs are too doleful. Somebody always a-dying for love, or a-killing somebody else, pushing people over cliffs, boats a-sinking on the sea with all hands lost. Makes a body feel like crying," Fern objected.

Nancy nudged Jodey. "Ask Grandpa Gruber if we'uns can be in the dance contest," she urged him.

Jodey waved his hand. "Grandpa Gruber," he began, "when you have the dance contest, Nancy and I want to know if we—"

"What kind of dancing are we supposed to do in this contest?" Fern interrupted.

"Why, square dancing," Grandpa Gruber replied. "What other kind? A real knockdown, drag-out square dance is always something to lighten the heart and lift the spirits."

Jodey sat down. "Wait a minute, let's see what they're going to decide," he whispered to Nancy. "If it's a square dance, they'll likely call on us."

Fern spoke up again. "Grandpa, we don't want the President to think we're back with Daniel Boone, a hundred years behind the times. All those old-timy things, turkey shoots and square dances and old ballads like Granny wants Aunt Rhoda to sing— they're plumb backwoodsy and out of date. We don't want the President to think we're ignoramuses here in the mountains—"

"No, we sure don't!" came a chorus of voices.

"I was thinking," Fern was encouraged to go on, "a jitterbug contest would be a lot better than a square dance contest."

"Jitterbug, what's that?" the mountain people looked puzzled. They glanced at each other. "She means a flitter bug, maybe, a lightning bug."

"Oh, I don't mean a real bug. The jitterbug's a kind of dance," Fern explained. "The young folks do it in Mountain City all the time. It's real exciting. You ought to see it. Daniel Mac-Murray there knows how to do it. He goes to the high school I go to, down in Mountain City."

"Get up and do us a measure, Fern. Let's see what this jitterbug is like," Grandpa suggested.

"You've got to have music," Fern said.

"I've got my fiddle along," Uncle Rufus offered.

"You've got to play boogiewoogie for us to dance the jitterbug," Fern answered.

Boogiewoogie—what was that? The mountain people looked at each other, mystified. They knew well enough what the boogie-*man* was—a black devil, with horns and a forked tail. But what was the boogiewoogie?

"It's a kind of music," Fern explained. "Mary Anne there can play it on the piano. If she'll play and Daniel will dance with me, I'll show you what the jitterbug is like."

Mary Anne Gruber seated herself at the school piano and the wild notes of boogiewoogie rang out. On the little platform Daniel and Fern began to jitterbug.

At first the people sat in frozen astonishment as Daniel and Fern pranced, Daniel throwing Fern into the air, catching her, Fern whirling away, to return and fly into the air again. After the first shock, all the folks laughed until the tears ran down their cheeks; they swayed and clapped with the jungle rhythm. When the performance finally came to an end there was a roar of applause.

At first it seemed that everybody was delighted with the

jitterbug, but as soon as people came to after the shock, there were loud shouts against it.

"All that jumping around—we'd look like a field full of grasshoppers!" Uncle Badger hollered.

"Oh Badger, you're an old stick-in-the-mud," Aunt Lizzie accused him. "I think that there jitterbug is the purtiest thing I ever saw!"

"I reckon you'd like to learn it," Uncle Badger exclaimed, "and go jumping around like a wild Indian with a red-hot coal in his shoe!"

"Maybe I would," Aunt Lizzie retorted. "I guess I can jump as high as the next one."

"What kind of music is that?" Uncle Rufus wanted to know. "Beating and banging on the keyboard! Sounds like just a lot of racket to me. A fiddle, now, has got tunes in it! It's got tunes that came up with the old folks through Cumberland Gap when the land was untrod by any but the savages."

Uncle Rufus put his fiddle to his shoulder and made a sound that sent shivers down people's backs. "There! You see, it's caught the sound of the Indian war whoop. And listen—" He made another sweep with his bow. "There's the cry of the cougar around the cabin door in the deep woods."

Everybody grew silent, remembering terrible tales they had heard of those lurking big cats, how they had attacked people as they walked along the trail at dusk or stolen toddling children from the very doors of the cabins.

Uncle Rufus played a lively snatch of *Arkansas Traveler* that brought smiles to their faces again and set their feet to tapping. "That's the kind of music we ought to have for the President," he cried. "Mountain music and a real lively square dance! It's been played for every square dance since 'way back yonder—"

"That's right, Uncle Rufus, that's right!" came shouts of encouragement.

Jodey stood up and waved his hat. "If you have this jitterbug contest, could Nancy and I do our jigs?"

"But we don't want to be old-timy, Uncle Rufus!" Fern cried. "The boogie and the jitterbug are new. They'd show we're keeping up with the times, that we're not shut away in the mountains without knowing a thing of what goes on in the world."

Shouts arose from all sides. "Fern's right. Let's have something new!"

"Don't give a durn about these newfangled ways. Give me a square dance every time!"

"No, no. We don't want the President to think we're back numbers. I'm for the jitterbug!"

Nancy and Jodey bounced up and frantically waved their hands. "How about our dances, too? Can't we do our dances?" they yelled. But with everyone else yelling for or against the jitterbug no one paid any attention to them.

Grandpa Gruber shouted for order. "Now, folks, no need to get het up. We'll take a vote and settle it that way. All that's for an old-time square dance hold up your hands!"

There was a silence as hands went up. Grandpa counted.

"Now, all that's for a jitterbug contest—"

A different set of hands arose and Grandpa counted again.

"Well, folks," he announced, "the jitterbugs have it by three votes."

Nancy looked at Jodey. "Now, while it's quiet," she prompted him. "Ask about ours."

"Grandpa Gruber," Jodey began, "what we want to know is can we—"

But the room was suddenly full of shouting.

"Them sassy-looking didoes to entertain the President!" Uncle Badger hollered. "Votes or no votes, I say it's outrageous!"

"We took a vote and won it, fair and democratic!" Fern shouted back.

"Yes, we sure did!" came cries of agreement.

"Democratic, democratic!" Uncle Badger yelled. "Always big words to settle things nowadays. I say that there boogie is buggy and I'm ready to shoot it out with anybody that wants to contradict me!"

"Shame on you, Badger!" Aunt Lizzie stood up and shook an angry finger. "I reckon you want to go back to feuding days, when folks had to settle things by shooting it out with a shotgun."

"Yi!" Jodey nudged Nancy. "They're a-going to fight!"

In the excitement Nancy forgot her own worry. Her eyes popped. What if they did begin shooting, like in the old days? She got ready to dodge under the desk.

The little schoolhouse seemed to rock and reel as everybody shouted at once. People banged on the desks and stamped with heavy brogans. Even the stove was bouncing and prancing on its legs.

Grandpa shouted for order, but no one paid any mind.

"If hit takes shooting to put a stop to this here bugging idea, I'm ready to shoot!" bawled Uncle Badger.

Jodey leaned toward Nancy. "Looks like they're all going buggy with the boogie," he snickered.

Nancy giggled.

Shaking his fists in the air, Uncle Badger accidentally struck the stovepipe which went up to the ceiling. It tottered. The others watched, holding their breath, but Uncle Badger, all unaware, went on shouting and vaporing. For a moment the stovepipe hung, then it parted and fell. Down it came with a terrific clatter, exactly on the top of Uncle Badger's head.

Soot spewed out in all directions. It fell in drifts on Uncle Badger and puffed out all over the room. Gasping and coughing, everybody rushed outside. What a sight they were—streaked and spotted with soot!

"Oh my stars, my clean percale!" mourned Granny Gruber, looking down at her dress.

"Just look at my new pink hair ribbon!" cried Ella.

"Gollies!" Jodey laughed at Nancy. "You're spotted as a wildcat."

"And you're streaked up like a coon," Nancy retorted.

The last to come out of the schoolhouse was a black man that no one recognized. People fell silent, staring, as he came tottering through the door. His eyes, peering out, looked like holes in a black mask. Who could it be? Then, with a start, they all recognized Uncle Badger.

"Now he's a boogie-man sure enough!" Mrs. MacMurray snickered. "All he needs is horns and a tail."

Everybody broke into howls of laughter.

"If I'm a boogie-man, you all better watch out," Uncle Badger growled. "Maybe I'll throw a spell on you!"

At that, everybody fell suddenly quiet. Nancy looked across at Dora. What if Uncle Badger *did* do witchcraft up there in his cave in the mountains after all? A scary feeling came over her. Then she shook it off. All that talk about witchcraft was just

foolishness—there was nothing to it.

"Now, folks, you see what you get for all those shines you cut in there," said Grandpa Gruber. "Hollering and stomping and talking about shooting it out. Looks to me like the Lord took a hand in this business. He gave a little tap on the head to the one that was the most at fault." He looked hard at Uncle Badger.

At these words, those who had shouted at the result of the voting looked down, shamefaced.

"Anybody now want to raise objections?" asked Grandpa. "Anybody feel like going home for his shotgun?"

Nobody made an answer.

"Then let's all go home, forget about the square dance, and do the best we can to make this jitterbug contest a ringtail rouser!"

"Humph!" said Uncle Badger.

Before Nancy and Jodey could gather their wits, people were scattering over the schoolyard, climbing onto their horses and into their jalopies and buggies and carts.

Nancy felt bewildered. "What'll we do now?" she asked Jodey blankly.

"Gollies, I don't know!" Jodey rumpled his hair till it looked like a witch's nest. "I sure don't know. Looks like it's too late to do anything."

A line of vehicles was streaming through the gate on the way toward home. Suddenly Nancy felt like crying. She turned away, glad that darkness was falling so that no one would see how disappointed she was. The biggest affair ever held in the mountains, and she and Jodey and the old-time dances were going to be left out.

# 3. Traipsing Round the Mountain

Across on Old Smoky the roosters were crowing. They were
answered by others on Razorback Ridge. The rosy glow of dawn
began to spread over the eastern sky. It stole through the
lavender blossoms of the catalpa tree outside Nancy's window
and lit up the little attic room where she lay asleep. She opened
her eyes slowly, wondering what it was that made her feel so
heavyhearted. Her glance strayed around the room. It went to
Mammy's medicinal herbs hanging from the rafters, to the sack
of hickory nuts stored in one corner, then fell on her soot-
streaked dress on the footboard of her bed where she had left
it after she took it off last night. Then it came to her. She and
Jodey had been left out of the big doin's for the dam—and all
those old-time dances at the tips of their toes!

Quickly she closed her eyes and hunched down into her squeaky shuck mattress. Better to be asleep than awake and thinking of something unhappy.

"Nance-e-e!" came a call, no louder than the distant crowing on the far mountain.

Nancy raised her head and listened.

It came again, "Nance-e-e!"

"It's Jodey!" She leaped out of bed, ran to the window and leaned out. "Hey, Jodey!" she shouted.

A veil of fog lay across the valley; she could see nothing of Old Smoky across the way except the highest ridges. Jodey's home was hidden in the mist, but his voice came over. "Hey, Nancy, I've got an idea!"

"An idea—about our dancing?"

"Sure thing!"

Nancy's spirits gave a happy leap. "Tell me!"

"Can't tell you now. It's something we'll have to keep mum about. Meet me at the crossroads in half an hour!"

"I'll be there!" Nancy drew her head in. And now someone else was shouting her name.

"Nance-e-e!" her mother's voice came up from below. "Time to get up. Hurry along. We need you!"

"Yes, Mammy!" Nancy put on her clothes and climbed down the ladder that led to the room below. There she found things in a tizzy.

Fern was rushing around like a hen with its head off. "How can we have a jitterbug contest when Daniel and Mary Anne are the only ones that know how? I'll have to go see them. We'll have to decide what to do about it. And all my chores to do! Mammy, couldn't I leave off my chores today?"

"Who's going to do 'em? I haven't got time." Mammy was emptying a bagful of dress scraps onto the table. "Now why didn't I tell the women to bring their scraps when they came this afternoon?" she mourned. "Not near enough here to make a quilt, not near enough. I'll have to send and tell 'em. Meanwhile I'd better press out these and have 'em ready to cut."

She set some irons on the hearth to heat. "I'll have to look up my patterns, too. And where are we going to get the cloth for the lining? Whose a-going to cook the breakfast? Nancy, honey, set the skillet on the fire and see if you can't cook breakfast while I do this ironing."

Nancy looked worried. How could she meet Jodey as she had promised if she was to cook breakfast? And there was that everlasting job of hauling up the water besides.

"Can't you skim the milk and make the butter for me today, Nancy?" cried Fern. "And sweep off the porches and feed the chickens? I've got to hustle round the mountain and see Mary Anne about this jitterbug contest."

Nancy's eyes flew open. She stared at her sister resentfully. If it hadn't been for all the excitement last night about the jitterbug contest, maybe someone would have listened when Jodey tried to speak about their old-time dances. For a long moment she stood looking at Fern's worried face.

"Oh, please do, Nancy," begged Fern. "Just look what a re-sponsibility I've got!"

"Well," Nancy frowned, considering. After all, they *had* voted to have the jitterbug contest and Grandpa Gruber had said that all were to do their part. "All right, Fern," she slowly agreed. "I'll help you out today." If she didn't get to the crossroads on time, like as not Jodey would wait or he would come on to the house.

"Thank you, honey. I'll help you out some time, wait and see!" Fern snatched up a piece of cold corn pone and rushed out of the door. "Mammy, I'm going!"

"You haven't had breakfast!" Mammy cried, but Fern was gone.

Nancy ran to the hearth to prepare the breakfast. She put some corn bread to bake in a skillet that stood on three legs over the fire. She shoveled some coals onto the cover so that the bread would bake on the top; then she put some bacon to fry in another skillet. It would be nice to have some eggs. She glanced at the egg basket on the shelf, then shook her head. Eggs weren't for eating, but to sell at the store for cash money. She dropped a piece of sassafras root into the kettle to boil for tea, then when everything was ready, she and Mammy and Pappy sat down at the smooth board table that Pappy had sawed long ago from a hickory log. Even though she had to eat in a hurry, the breakfast tasted good, especially with the wild honey to go on their bread. She gulped the last of her hot sassafras tea and excused herself. There was so much to do.

She ran out to feed the chickens. At the barn she scooped up a measure of corn and gave it a scattering toss.

"Chick, chick, chick!" she yelled. The chickens came running.

She closed the barn door, ran for the broom, gave the porch a lick and a promise, then began to draw up the water. There was no hurrying that, the buckets were too heavy. They came up slowly as Nancy hauled and hauled away. By the time she got to the eighth one, the sun was halfway up the eastern sky. It must be going on ten o'clock. She wondered if Jodey was still waiting. Maybe he'd think she wasn't coming and would go home.

Nancy hustled into the kitchen, skimmed the cream, and poured it into the churn. She began to bang the dasher up and down. That was another long job. She churned furiously until she was out of breath and red in the face. Every five minutes she looked into the churn to see if the butter had come. At last she saw a yellow blob of it at the bottom. There now, everything was finished. Now she could meet Jodey at the crossroads!

She set the churn on the kitchen table and ran out of the back door. She had almost reached the gate when Mammy called her. "Wait a minute there, where are you going?"

"Down the road a piece to meet Jodey."

"You can't go now. I've got some errands for you to do."

Nancy groaned. She turned and came slowly back to the house.

"Get the splint basket down from the rafters," Mammy directed. "I want you to go round to the neighbors' houses and gather up some quilt scraps. Stop at Dora's house first and ask Aunt Lizzie for some, then go along to the mill. After that, go to Uncle Rufus' house and then on to Granny Gruber's. Tell 'em all to send along their scraps and I'll get 'em all ironed out so they can be cut out this afternoon."

On hearing what the errand was, Nancy brightened. She'd have to go by the crossroads where Jodey was, to get to the mill. She took the basket and raced through the gate and along the road to Dora's house.

Aunt Lizzie was nowhere to be seen, but Nancy found Dora in the kitchen, bending over a huge brass preserving kettle, stirring and stirring a bubbling mass of strawberries. Her little face was flushed and perspiring.

"Hey there, Dora, where's Aunt Lizzie?" Nancy asked.

"Aunt Lizzie? Goodness only knows where she is. She hollered for me a while ago like she'd seen a witch. She stuck the spoon in my hand and told me to cook the preserves. Then she took off down the road like somebody was sticking her with pins. Whatever struck her I don't know. She thinks a mighty heap of these preserves, spent all day yesterday picking the berries on the mountains and she knows well I don't know anything about making preserves. All I know is you shouldn't let 'em stick to the bottom and burn. I'm that bothered I don't know what to do."

Nancy stood a moment puzzling over Dora's story, then she inquired, "Do you reckon Aunt Lizzie would mind if you gave me some scraps for the President's quilt?"

"Go in the shed-room there and open the big chest. They're in there. Just take what you want."

Nancy found the chest and selected the scraps she liked best. At the bottom she came upon some yellow linen neatly folded. There seemed to be many yards of it. "It's as yellow as the dandelions that come up in the springtime," Nancy stood gazing at it admiringly. Then she lifted it from the chest and held it up at the kitchen door. "What's this, Dora?"

"I don't know. It's been there long as I can remember."

"I was a-thinking. It would make a heavenly lining for the President's quilt."

"Take it," Dora said recklessly. "What good is it doing lying there at the bottom of that chest year after year?"

Nancy laid the linen in her basket and took her leave.

"If you meet up with Aunt Lizzie anywhere along the way," Dora called after her, "tell her she'd better come home and see about these strawberries. I can't tell when they're done."

"I'll tell her." Nancy hurried away.

At the crossroads there was not a sign of Jodey. Nancy was standing under a spreading chestnut tree, looking anxiously around her when a fierce snarl like that of a wildcat sounded from the thick branches above.

Quick as a flash, she leaped from beneath the branches. There was a sound of something hurtling through the leaves. She was just ready to fly away when a pair of skinny legs in blue jeans swung down from a limb followed by a plaid shirt, then the grinning face of Jodey.

"Land sakes! Can't you ever show up without scaring a body outen her wits!" Nancy exclaimed.

Jodey laughed. "That's what you get for being so late. I made up a song with sixteen verses while I was waiting. I thought you weren't coming at all."

Nancy explained why she was late, then she exclaimed, "What's the idea you told me about? Have you thought of some way for us to get to do our dances at the affair?"

"No, I haven't," Jodey replied. "Not exactly."

Nancy was disappointed. "What was it then—your idea?"

"Well—" Jodey rumpled his hair until it stood up like porcupine

quills. "You know how Uncle Badger is. He's full of ideas. He remembers things handed down from the time of Daniel Boone. And he thinks up curious and different ways of doing things. If he put his head to it, I'm sure he could tell us just what we could do to get into that contest. My idea was to go up there to his cave today and ask him to help us out."

"But—but—you know what they say about Uncle Badger. I'm afeared. If he *is* a witchman, he'll be mad as a hornet to have us come poking around up there. Why, we might come on him when he's making a spell or something."

"Shucks, that's all foolishness—just old superstitions. Uncle Badger is just sharper than other folks and when he beats 'em at something like snaring rabbits or shooting at marks or finding honey, they just say he does it by witchcraft."

"Well—" Nancy looked down at the road; she kicked uneasily at a dirt clod. "Anyway, I couldn't go today. I've got some errands to do. Mammy's sent me traipsing around to get quilt scraps. I've got to go to the mill and to Uncle Rufus' and then on to Granny Gruber's house."

"I'll go with you. Uncle Badger's cave is in that mountain up above Granny Gruber's house. It's right along the way, not far off the road. I know how to get there. We'll stop off; it won't take long. Come on."

Nancy felt frightened but she set off with Jodey for the mill. The road led along the edge of a mountain. On one side the cliffs towered high above them and on the other, the land fell away and there was nothing but the air and sky. Down below the valley was spread out all blue and shimmery with the distance. The houses looked like little matchboxes with roads like tiny ribbons leading among them. It was a pretty sight and a beautiful bright day. Nancy took some deep breaths of the cool mountain air and began to feel braver.

"This here's the song I made up while I was a-waiting." Jodey began to sing. His merry voice went echoing among the high cliffs and rang out over the valley:

> Way up on old Smoky where folks seldom go,
> We lost an old bruin for shooting too slow.
> For shooting too slow, boys, for shooting too slow.
> We missed an old bruin for shooting too slow.

A waterfall tumbling over the cliff made a splashing, crashing noise and Jodey broke off. He waited until the falls were well behind them and the stream had quieted to a bubbling creek that flowed along beside the road, then he sang a second verse:

> I met that old bruin inside of a tree.
> He came to get honey, but thought he'd take me.
> He thought he'd take me, boys, he thought he'd take me.
> He came to get honey, but thought he'd—

Jodey suddenly stopped singing. He turned his head, listening. A strange booming sound was in the air.

"What's that?" Nancy heard it too.

Boom, boom, boom! The noise was savage and wild.

"What in all get-out? It sounds like Indian drums!" Jodey looked at Nancy with startled eyes.

"Can't be," Nancy shook her head. "There haven't been any Indians around here for a hundred years."

"There's Cherokees over the line in North Carolina, a whole settlement of 'em," Jodey said.

"Shucks, they've taken to farming and making baskets for the tourists. They don't get out beating drums and going on the war-path any more."

Boom, boom, boom, boom, boom! The noise went on and on. It seemed to grow louder as the children came nearer the mill. Up the road, beyond the small house where the MacMurrays lived, they could see the mill with its great wheel standing idle. That was queer, for usually on weekdays, when Mr. MacMurray was grinding corn, the wheel went over and over, turned by the weight of water that splashed and sparkled over it from the millstream. But they were too perplexed by the booming sound to think about it at the moment. They walked on, peering warily around for whatever mysterious thing could be causing the noise.

As they came to the MacMurray house, they learned what it was. At the corner of the house, where the gutters led down to the rain barrel, stood Mrs. MacMurray. She was beating on the barrel with an old ax handle.

Boom, boom, boom! The hollow thunder went out to the hill-sides and echoed back again.

Jodey and Nancy stood staring. What could be the matter with Mrs. MacMurray? Why was she standing there banging away on the rain barrel?

"Maybe she's trying to call rain outen the sky," Nancy said. "It *has* been mighty dry lately. I can't see any other reason why she should be doing it." Mrs. MacMurray looked so grim they didn't dare to speak to her.

Jodey shook his head in perplexity. "We'll go into the mill and find Mr. MacMurray and ask *him*," he said.

They climbed the steps to the mill and peered uneasily through the open door. What they saw made them feel more bewildered than before. Mr. MacMurray was there, jumping around the floor like a frog out of his own millpond. White flour dust flew up from the floor boards as he stomped with his heavy

brogans. His hair and shoulders were white with it. He caught sight of the children standing in the doorway.

"No meal today, no grinding. I can't stop, I can't stop!" he bawled at them.

Jodey and Nancy turned and left the mill hastily.

"What ails 'em?" cried Nancy.

"They must've gone crazy—stark, starin' crazy!" Jodey said.

"Let's go to the house and find Bluett. Maybe she can tell us what's happened," Nancy suggested.

They ran up the path to the house. At the back Mrs. Mac-Murray was still banging away at the barrel. They knocked on the door. Bluett MacMurray let them in. She was covered with a large checked apron and her blue eyes were bulging like onions.

"Bluett!" Nancy exclaimed. "What's the matter with your mammy and pappy?"

"I don't know!" Bluett answered. "They were all right at breakfast. Right afterwards, Mammy sent me out on the mountains to look for some poke salad greens. We were all a-hankering for something fresh—been eating leather-britches all winter long——" she pointed at a garland of dried stringbeans hanging on the wall, each split to look like a tiny pair of breeches. "I was gone about an hour. When I came back, there was Mammy out behind the house pounding the rain barrel like she was bewitched and Pappy was there in the grinding room, jumping up and down like he didn't know how to stop. When I asked Mammy what she was a-doing, she yelled at me to get along in the house and cook the greens. I've got 'em on there in the pot with an old ham bone and some corn meal dumplings." Bluett pointed to the hearth where a black iron pot hung over the fire.

Then she leaned toward Jodey and Nancy and suddenly whispered, "You know what I think?"

"What?"

"I think they've been 'witched!"

Nancy gasped.

"Yes, I do. Did you ever hear 'bout the time Cousin Matt Huggins was out in the woods hunting? He was real thirsty and about that time along came an old red cow. He got the idea he'd milk her and drink the milk, but when he put his hand on her side to make her stand still, it stuck there and he couldn't get it off. And that cow ran over the hills and through the briars and bushes and Cousin Matt had to run with her. She ran till she came to——" Bluett broke off and looked fearfully over her shoulder.

"To—to—what?" Jodey prompted.

"To Uncle Badger's cave," Bluett whispered. "It was *his* cow! Anyway, that's the tale Cousin Matt told when he got home. Oh, he was scratched up a sight," Bluett nodded at them knowingly. Then she glanced over her shoulder and continued whispering. "You remember what Uncle Badger said yesterday, when he came out of the schoolhouse all black with soot? Everybody laughed at him and he said, 'Watch out, maybe I'll throw a spell on you.'" She bobbed her head at her pop-eyed visitors. "Well, I think that's just what he's done!"

Nancy and Jodey stood silent, too flabbergasted for words. Nancy's thoughts flew back to what Dora had said about Aunt Lizzie: "She hollered for me like she'd seen a witch." And then a little later: "She took off down the road like somebody was sticking her with pins." Wasn't that the way people felt who had been bewitched?

She told Bluett and Jodey what Dora had said.

"Uh-huh! Aunt Lizzie too!" Bluett exclaimed. "I've heard tell that a witch can make a little clay statue of a body, stick it all full of pins and then that person will feel the pain—just where the pins are stuck in the statue."

Nancy glanced at Jodey. He looked worried. Well, witches or not, she thought, she had to do Mammy's errand. She explained to Bluett what she had come for.

"There are plenty of scraps in the rag bag," Bluett said. She brought a white flour sack and emptied it on the bed.

Nancy gathered what she wanted, then she and Jodey said good-by.

"If your ma and pa don't get better real soon," Nancy said, "maybe you'd better go see Grandpa Gruber. They say he knows how to handle witches."

Nancy glanced sideways at Jodey as they walked along the road to Uncle Rufus' house. "Maybe we'd better give up the idea of going to the cave."

"If he's a witch, all the more reason to go," Jodey declared. "If he's a witch, he can sure as shooting get us into the dance contest. He'd only have to throw a spell and *make* it happen."

"He might throw a spell on us. Maybe he'd put us to jumping up and down or running through the briars. Anyway, it's getting too late to go," Nancy squinted up at the sun. "It's a far piece around the mountain to Uncle Rufus' house and then on to Granny Gruber's. I'd not get back before afternoon."

"We don't have to go the long way by the road," Jodey pointed out. "We can climb straight up over the mountain. 'T ain't far that way."

Nancy glanced up the shaggy mountainside. "All right then,"

she reluctantly agreed. She didn't want Jodey to think she was a coward.

It was a hard climb. They struggled over stones and ledges and through mats of white-flowering blackberry bushes. Small lizards with bright blue throats flashed away from their feet to hide in stony crevices, and once a rabbit jumped up and darted off into the underbrush. The sun shone out bright and hot. Grasshoppers leaped away on all sides. Finally they saw the backbone of the mountain just above them.

"I'm as hot as a roasted potato!" Nancy paused and wiped her perspiring face with the end of her skirt.

"It's not far now," Jodey said. "Just over the hump and there we are!"

They thought pleasantly of Uncle Rufus' little cabin where they could rest in the shade on the quiet porch. "Maybe Aunt Hettie will give us a glass of cold buttermilk from the springhouse," Nancy said.

"Whoopee! Let's go!" Inspired by the suggestion, Jodey went up the steep slopes in a burst of new energy. Uncle Rufus' little mountain farm was just over the ridge.

When at last they reached the top of the mountain, they breathed a sigh of relief. They looked down on the little cluster of buildings on the other side and stopped stock-still, gaping with astonishment.

"What in the land of the living!" gasped Nancy.

Uncle Rufus' pack of hunting dogs sat with heads in the air, howling dismally. The cows were at the gate, mooing in a distracted way. Mingling with these sounds was a strange squealing noise that sounded like a pig with the stomach-ache.

Nancy and Jodey went slipping and sliding down the moun-

tain until they were in Uncle Rufus' back yard. Through the
kitchen window they could hear Ella shouting at Great-aunt
Hettie who was quite deaf.

"No, no, Auntie, I didn't say they'd been switched," they
could hear her yelling above the howling and mooing and
squealing.

"They've been switched?" Auntie shouted back. "That's what
I *thought* you said. Is that why they're all bawling and carrying
on so? Who switched 'em, that's what I want to know?"

"Nobody's switched 'em, Auntie!"

"Somebody's switched 'em? Did they switch your Uncle Rufus, too? What's he doing making that awful squealing with his
fiddle? Did they switch him, too?"

"No, no, Auntie, not switched, I said 'witched. Somebody's
'witched 'em."

Nancy looked at Jodey. Here too! Now she was sure Uncle
Badger was a witchman and had laid a spell on everybody on
Razorback Ridge. "Maybe we shouldn't go in," she said doubt-
fully. "But how'll I get Mammy's quilt scraps?"

Just then Ella and Aunt Hettie came out and greeted them.
"Come in, if you can stand the racket," Ella said.

"Somebody's been around and switched all the critters,"
Auntie said. "They're a-carrying on fit to kill. I'm that tired of
the racket I feel like running away to the woods. But come in
and sit a spell, if you've a mind to."

"We haven't got time to stop, Auntie," Nancy shouted. "I just
came to get some quilt scraps."

"What say—killed Pap?" Auntie leaned toward her in alarm.
"Who killed Pap? You mean *your* pappy?"

"No, no, Auntie. Nobody's killed Pappy. I said quilt scraps, QUILT SCRAPS!"

"Oh, *quilt scraps!* Why didn't you say so in the first place? You gave me a real bad scare. You ought not to go round scaring people, saying somebody's killed your pappy. Besides, hit's bad luck." She went into the house and brought out an armful of scraps which she put into Nancy's basket. "Just as soon as I get dinner on, I'm a-going over to see Grandpa Gruber and see if anybody's been switching *their* animals."

Ella threw up her hands in despair. "I was trying to tell her I thought the critters had all been 'witched. And Uncle Rufus, too. I'm a-going over to Grandpa Gruber's myself. They say he's a witch-master and knows how to kill a witch with a silver bullet. That's the only way it can be done."

Nancy looked at Jodey in a frightened way. She didn't want Uncle Badger to be killed, witchman or not. "We'll be a-leaving," she said to Ella and Auntie. "We'll see you at Grandpa Gruber's, maybe."

The Grubers lived in a whitewashed cabin at the end of the cove. As they hurried along the trail, Nancy and Jodey could see it shining among the green trees. Behind it the shaggy wall of the mountain rose up to the clouds. It was so high that Grandpa Gruber always said he could look up the chimney and watch the cows a-grazing on the slopes above. When Nancy and Jodey came to a small path that went zigging and zagging upward, Jodey stopped and pointed.

"Up there's Uncle Badger's cave."

Nancy peered up at the frowning cliffs. Her heart sank, but Jodey was already mounting the path, so she took a good breath and followed. The narrow trail went higher and higher. At one place it curved around the mountain above Grandpa Gruber's house. They looked down onto the yard and stopped in shocked surprise. Furniture was strewn all over the lawn. Beds stood this way and that. An old corner cupboard leaned crazily under an oak tree. Chairs, chests, and benches were scattered about.

"Look at their house plunder," Nancy exclaimed. "What's happened?"

"They're a-moving, maybe."

"Where would they move to? The Grubers have lived here since Daniel Boone fought the Indians. They're not a-going to move nowhere."

"Maybe they couldn't make the payments on their plunder," Jodey suggested. "Maybe the storeman's come to take it back to the store."

"Why no, that's all homemade stuff. It's old as the hills. Grandpa Gruber made it himself when he and Granny were first married. I heard her say so."

For a long moment they stood staring down on the confusion in the yard below. If it wasn't witchcraft that had the mountain community topsy-turvy, what could it be? Aunt Lizzie rushing off leaving her preserves to ruin, running down the road as if stuck with pins. Mrs. MacMurray behind the house beating the rain barrel, Mr. MacMurray jumping up and down in a cloud of flour dust. All the animals stirred up at Uncle Rufus', the cows a-bawling, the dogs a-howling, and Uncle Rufus himself making squalling noises on his fiddle that fairly made a body's ears split. And now here was Grandpa Gruber's house plunder hauled out and scattered over the yard. If it wasn't witchcraft what had happened?

Nancy grasped Jodey's arm. "I'm a-telling you. I think we ought not to go."

"Stay here if you're afeard," Jodey said. "I'm a-going." He stalked on.

Nancy decided to follow. Just in front of them the path led into a dark cleft. The mountain was split apart leaving a narrow space between and they had to go single-file on the path. Nancy followed fearfully in Jodey's footsteps. It grew darker and darker in the cleft as they went along. Its walls were taller and taller. Far up above, only a streak of light showed. The walls were wet with oozing water and felt slimy to their hands. At one place something scuttled across the path in front of their feet. In the gloom they only caught a glimpse of it as it slid into a hole in the rocks. Was it a lizard or was it a snake? Nancy thought of the bright sunshine outside. Oh, why had she come into this black tunnel? What would happen to them before they got out of it? Her heart was thumping against her ribs. Then, just as she felt she would die of fright, the path widened.

They came upon a clear space about as wide as the barnyard at home. The rocky walls of the mountain stood up all around it. Trees and bushes leaned over the top so that the light entered only dimly with a greenish cast. It was like being in a great stone fortress. Before them was a wooden door set into the mountainside. It was tight shut.

"This must be Uncle Badger's cave," Jodey whispered.

Nancy stood back, holding her breath. Jodey tiptoed up to the door and knocked. Slowly it opened—but only a crack. A gun barrel came poking through.

"Who's there?" a voice challenged them.

Jodey goggled at the gun. "It—it's me, Jodey Calloway, and Nancy's with me."

At that the door opened wider, the gun was lowered and Uncle Badger looked out.

"My gollies, young'uns. Where are your raisings? What kind of manners is that, coming knocking on the door without giving a whoop and a holler? Don't you know it's polite to stand off a ways and holler, to let a man know whether it's friend or foe? That's the way proper folks did in the old times and it's a good custom still."

"Y-y-yes, sir, Uncle Badger," stammered Jodey.

Uncle Badger shoved the door open and came out. Nancy gasped. She grabbed Jodey's arm and pulled him a step backward. Uncle Badger had a broom in his hand—and horrors!—his arms were blackened to the elbows.

Uncle Badger, following her eyes, glanced down at his broom and his blackened arms.

"Don't wonder you're shocked," he said, laughing. "Been cleaning out the chimney," he pointed to a length of stovepipe sticking out of the side of the mountain near the door. "Them pesky chimney swallows are always a-setting in there building their nests. First thing I know, my whole cave is full of smoke and there are the pore little birds half dead with it. Every once in a while I have to run a broom up the chimney and shove their nests out." He pointed to the ground beneath the protruding stovepipe. A broken bird's nest did indeed lie there. Evidently it had been pushed out of the pipe.

Nancy breathed a sigh of relief.

"Got a real nice place here, haven't I, young'uns?" Uncle Badger gestured around the rock-walled clearing. "In the summer when it's hot outside, it's as cool as a cucumber here. And in the winter when the wind blows like old scratch, ne'er a breeze can get in. Hit's as snug as a bug in a rug. Over there in that 'there cave across the way is where I keep my cow and my old mule for plowing. And in here are my own diggings. Wait just a minute and I'll show 'em to you."

Uncle Badger went to a small stream that trickled through the rock and washed his arms. Then he pushed open the door of the cave. Nancy entered, followed by Jodey. The cave was small. Uncle Badger had whitewashed the rocky walls so that they shone clean and white. A bed in one corner was covered with a bright patchwork quilt. A fireplace with a stovepipe chimney had been built on one side and there were some ladder-backed chairs and a table. It was neat and cozy and there was no sign of anything that looked like witchcraft.

Jodey began to explain to Uncle Badger why they had come. "We thought maybe you could think up some way to get us into that dance contest," he said. "We want to do our old-time jigs. But seems like everybody at the meeting got so het up about the jitterbug business they didn't give us a chance to speak. And now we don't know what to do about it."

Uncle Badger pondered a while. "Folks have already voted to have the jitterbug contest," he finally spoke up. "And as Fern said, they won it fair and democratic. 'Course I got a little het up the other day and went to hollering a whole lot of foolishness. But what she said was right, if you come right down to facts. It wouldn't be fair and democratic to just poke your dances into the program without taking a vote on it. You've got to have the permission of all," he paused, looking down at his old rawhide shoes. "Well, not all," he corrected himself. "But the majority. That's to

say, you ought to have the permission of more than half the
folks that were at the meeting."

"But Uncle Badger, how can we get folks' permission? They're
not going to have another meeting."

"There's a way," Uncle Badger said, positively.

"There is? What is it?" Jodey and Nancy looked at him
eagerly.

"There's always a way to do everything," Uncle Badger said.
"If you can think of it and if you don't mind work."

"What is it?"

The old man tipped his head and glanced at Nancy slyly. "Do
you know how to do any witchcraft?"

Nancy gave a start. Her eyes opened wide. "N-no, no, sir,"
she stammered.

"Maybe you could try," said Uncle Badger. "It's a thing that
requires witchcraft!"

Nancy looked frightened, but Jodey spoke up at once. "I'd
be willing to try!"

"Oh, I bet you would," said Uncle Badger. "You'd try to haul
a wildcat outen his hole if a body suggested it. Fact is, I think
you know some witchcraft already, both of you. Don't you know
how to make a piece of paper talk?"

"Piece of paper talk! What do you mean, Uncle Badger?"
Nancy and Jodey both spoke at once.

Uncle Badger got up and went to a crevice in the rock wall
where he had stuffed some odds and ends, cans full of nails, balls
of twine, paper bags full of this and that. He took out a pencil
and a writing tablet. "This here is what I mean. When a body
takes a piece of paper and makes marks on it and somebody else
can look at it and get a message from it, that looks like witch-

craft to me. I can't do it. But I allus have the hankering to. I keep this here tablet and pencil here, thinking maybe I'll learn it, but somehow I never get around to it."

"Oh, you mean writing!" Nancy said.

"Sure. That's the strongest kind of witchcraft there is," Uncle Badger handed her the tablet. "Now you take this paper and make a witch spell with it and maybe it'll get you into the dance contest. I'll tell you just what to make it say."

Nancy and Jodey laughed like loons. Nancy took the paper and pencil and pulled her chair up to the table. "What'll I make it say, Uncle Badger?"

The old man cleared his throat. "Make it say this: 'We, the undersigned, do petition—' "

Nancy wrote carefully.

Uncle Badger kept on. " '—and ask that Jodey and Nancy Calloway do perform their old-time jigs in the dance contest at the big doin's for the dam.' That's all."

"That's all?" echoed Jodey and Nancy blankly.

"Well, you have to take the paper around and get folks to sign their names on it. If you can get maybe twenty-five or thirty names, that's the same as getting a winning vote."

"That shouldn't be hard!" Nancy cried in surprise.

"Easy as falling off a log!" Jodey exclaimed.

"Well, you see it pays to know a little witchcraft," Uncle Badger said. "Wish I knowed some! Come to think of it, maybe you better add a little persuasion there on that paper. Put this on at the bottom: 'We, the undersigned, do think it a good idea to have both kinds of dances at the doin's, the new kind to show we're right up-to-date and the old kind to show we've not forgotten our past and are proud of it.' "

Nancy took down the words.

"And that's all there is to it," Uncle Badger said. "Now you take the paper around and see if you can't get folks to sign it. When you get your twenty-five or thirty names on it, you take the paper to Grandpa Gruber. He's in charge of the affair. And he'll put you right on the program."

"We can stop at all the houses on the way home and get names," said Nancy.

"No chance of getting any names any place today," Jodey answered. "Everybody seems to have gone clean hog-wild here on Razorback Ridge." He and Nancy interrupted each other telling Uncle Badger about the strange goings-on they had discovered along the way.

The old man looked puzzled. "What in tarnation can be the matter?" he said, pondering.

"And when we passed above Grandpa Gruber's house to come up here," Jodey went on, "there was all their house plunder out in the yard, scattered every which way."

"Something real bad must've happened," Uncle Badger exclaimed. "I better go see if I can do something. Come on, young-'uns, let's go!" He seized his gun from a corner and rushed out of the door. The children ran at his heels. They hurried through the dark cleft, then along the trail above the Gruber house. The furniture was still scattered helter-skelter about the yard. Not a soul was to be seen, but squalling noises came floating up to them.

"It looks queer, for a fact," Uncle Badger exclaimed. "And sounds queer, too!" He hurried down the zigzagging trail. As they came to Grandpa Gruber's gate, they met Aunt Hettie and Ella coming out.

"What's the trouble here, how come all their plunder's out in the yard?" Uncle Badger asked.

"Why, hit's a plague of the seven-year locusts," Auntie exclaimed. "They're a-trying to get rid of 'em, I reckon."

"No, no, Auntie, that ain't what they said!" Ella shook her head. "You didn't hear 'em right."

Uncle Badger and the children looked toward the house. On the porch rail the geranium pots were bouncing up and down. The strings of red peppers hanging against the wall were jouncing. The little house itself was shaking with the bumping and thumping that seemed to be going on inside. Nancy recognized the sound of the Gruber's old reed organ, mingled with a strange medley of twangs, bangs, and squeaks from other musical instruments.

"Last time we had a plague of locusts, they came in a cloud," Aunt Hettie went on. "They et up the cornfields and the garden sass and even the leaves off the trees. They left everything as bare as the palm of my hand. I'm a-telling you, all that jumping around in there ain't going to scare 'em off. And that music racket ain't going to do no good, either. They'd better get out and start a backfire. Burn 'em out and smoke 'em out, that's the only way."

"Auntie, 't ain't no plague, 't ain't no locusts!" bawled Ella above all the noise that was coming from the Gruber house.

"But they said it was little bugs—"

"No, no, Auntie. Not *little* bugs—jitterbugs!"

"A plague of jitterbugs?" Auntie leaned forward with one hand to her ear.

"Oh my!" Ella cast her eyes upward with a hopeless expression.

A look of understanding came over Nancy's face. "Oh! They're all in there practicing the jitterbug, is that it?

"That's what they're a-doing. They moved out all the furniture so they'd have room to dance."

So that was it! Nancy and Jodey and Uncle Badger looked at each other. They began to understand what had set the mountain community topsy-turvy.

"That must be what's the matter with the dogs at home," Aunt Hettie spoke up. "And the cows. Them jitterbugs must be biting 'em something terrible."

"No, no, Auntie," Ella shouted. "I asked Ma in there about it. The dogs are a-howling because Uncle's fiddle music hurts their ears. He's a-practicing to play for the jitterbugs. Fern was at our house this morning and she said they had to have a boogie-woogie band. Everybody that could play any kind of instrument had to be in it, she said. So Uncle Rufus went to practicing and the dogs went to howling. They always howl like that when he plays high notes. The cows are a-bawling because Pappy and Mammy hurried off with Fern to learn the jitterbug and forgot to milk 'em. I reckon they're so full of milk they're fit to bust."

Although Auntie bent toward Ella with a hand behind her ear, she didn't catch a word of this explanation. She turned to Nancy. "You watch out for them jitterbugs on the way home," she warned. "They might begin biting *you*. Have you got any of them jitterbugs at your house?" she inquired of Jodey.

"Sure have, Auntie," Jodey yelled. "They seem to be all over the mountains."

"Awful plague, awful!" Auntie shook her head.

Nancy stared toward the house. Through the window she could see Mrs. Gruber madly pumping the organ. Sitting beside her was Aunt Lizzie, twanging away as she blew on a jew's-harp, her old face puckered like a dry persimmon. Aunt Rhoda was seated with them, stroking the dulcimer fit to kill. And there on the other side of the organ was Mrs. MacMurray, frowning and grim, boom-boom-booming away on a big bass drum. Jitterbugs kept passing and repassing in front of the door, jumping and bouncing and cavorting. Nancy caught a glimpse of Mary Anne stamping around with someone whose back was to the door. They turned and she recognized Mr. MacMurray, his coat still full of flour dust.

So that was the explanation! Fern had been around early organizing a boogiewoogie band and giving lessons in jitterbugging. At this moment Fern came rushing out of the door and along the path. She grabbed Uncle Badger by the arm.

"You're just the person we've been a-looking for, Uncle Badger. Where's your banjo? Do, for the land's sake, go home and get it. We need you to play in the boogiewoogie band!" She turned him about and gave him a little push up the mountain.

Though a mite startled, Uncle Badger kept going, striding along in a great hurry. "I'll be back in three jerks," he called to Fern.

"Awful plague, awful," Auntie shook her head again. "Just look how they're jumping around in there—it's awful!"

"I'll say it is, Auntie," Nancy howled fervently. Then she turned to Jodey. "Anyway, I'll ask Granny for some quilt scraps."

"And we'll get some names on our paper!" Jodey exclaimed. "Just look how many folks are here—twenty-five if there's a one. Maybe we can get all the names at once. Then we can speak to Grandpa Gruber and we'll be in the contest!"

"Oh, that would be just grand! When they stop dancing we'll ask 'em."

But it began to look as if the jitterbugs weren't going to stop dancing. Nancy and Jodey waited and waited. They shifted from one foot to another. They sat down. They stood up. Uncle Badger came with his banjo and joined the boogiewoogie band. Still there was not a pause.

"It's a-getting late. Mammy will be expecting me," Nancy said. "Suppose I go in and ask for the quilt scraps. Maybe that'll put Mrs. Gruber in the notion to call a halt."

"Go on," Jodey urged.

Nancy peered in at the cabin door. All the young folks and half of the old ones of Razorback Ridge were there, all leaping and bouncing and whirling. The only thing in the room that seemed in its right mind and going about its business as usual was the old iron cooking pot. It hung in the chimney, bubbling away, and Nancy could smell the ham and turnip greens cooking inside it. She ventured into the cabin, dodged the leaping jitterbugs, and reached Mrs. Gruber who was still playing the organ. She pulled at her sleeve.

"Excuse me, Mrs. Gruber. Mammy sent me to ask for some quilt scraps—"

Mrs. Gruber shook her head. "Run along, run along, honey. I can't be bothered now!"

Nancy drew back. Then looking around, she caught sight of Mary Anne Gruber jumping around with Mr. MacMurray and shouting instructions. Nancy caught her arm. "Oh, please Mary Anne—" she began. "Mammy wants some—"

"Some other time, some other time!" Mary Anne pranced away.

Nancy began to feel discouraged. Then she thought, "There's still Granny Gruber. Maybe she'll listen." She peered around the room and finally spied Granny with the boogiewoogie band. She was blowing the harmonica, her old cheeks puffed out like a squirrel's stuffed with nuts.

But Granny was no more to be distracted than the others. "Not now, not now!" she exclaimed impatiently when Nancy spoke to her, and went on blowing the harmonica.

Nancy went back to Jodey. "They won't pay me any mind," she said. "What'll we do? They're so took up with their dancing they just won't take any notice."

"I'll make 'em take notice," Jodey said. "Get ready with that paper. I'll roust 'em out of there!" He snatched a string of red peppers from the wall and hung it around his neck. Then before Nancy had time to ask questions, he went clambering up one corner of the log cabin. He scrambled onto the roof and scampered over the old split shingles. When he came to the chimney he took the dry peppers from around his neck and crumbled them with his hands. Then he tossed them into the chimney.

Almost immediately a rash of sneezing broke out inside the house. "Ah-choo, ker-chuff!" The harmonica and dulcimer fell silent. "Er-chow, ah-choo!" The noise of stamping and bounding changed to one of coughing and sneezing. Then, like sheep stampeding through a broken fence, everybody rushed out of the cabin. Their faces were red and their eyes watering.

· "A-a-ah, o-o-oh!" they gasped, trying to catch their breath. "What happened all of a sudden? I was choking to death—ah-choo, ah-chuff!" "Oh, this air feels good!" Gradually people came to themselves.

Granny Gruber leaned against the pillar of the porch. "Why, hi there, Nancy, where'd you come from?"

"Mammy sent me to ask you to send over some quilt scraps—" Nancy began.

"Quilt scraps? Why yes, child." Granny looked over the furniture scattered in the yard. She crossed over to an old pine chest and brought out an armful of bright pieces. "Take 'em all." She stuffed them into Nancy's basket.

"And another thing I wanted to ask you, Granny—" Nancy took out the paper Uncle Badger had dictated.

But on the porch people had begun to ask who could have thrown the red pepper onto the fire.

"You did that, Daniel, it's just like you!" Fern accused.

"I never!" Daniel cried.

Loud voices rose, everybody accusing everybody else. "You did that!" "No, I never. You did it yourself!" Then they caught sight of Jodey climbing down from the roof.

"He's the one. And there's Nancy. Those two—they did it! Come on, we'll give them something to make *them* sneeze!" Everyone rushed to catch Jodey and Nancy.

Jodey dashed across the yard. He seized Nancy's arm. "Come on, come on!" he yelled.

"But our paper—" cried Nancy. "The names on our paper!"

The jitterbugs came charging toward them. "We'll give that Jodey a good trouncing—and Nancy, too!"

Nancy and Jodey dashed through the gate and flew down the trail. For a while the jitterbugs ran after them, then they gave up the chase and went back to their dancing.

"Now see what happened!" Nancy cried as they slowed to a walk. "You had to go and throw red pepper onto the fire! Now how'll we get our paper signed? We'll never find so many people all together again."

"Shucks." Jodey was untroubled. "There are more ways than one to skin a cat. Aren't all the ladies going to meet at your house this afternoon?"

"Why, yes, they are," said Nancy brightening.

"Then why worry? You can ask them all to sign their names. That'll do it!"

"Sure and certain!" Nancy's spirits rose again. "I can get them all this afternoon." She set off for home with her basket piled high with quilt scraps, while Jodey took a short cut to his own cabin on Smoky Mountain.

# 4. *The Delectable Mountains*

When Nancy arrived home, Pappy was washing his face and hands at the shelf on the back porch. Mammy was hurriedly ladling out the dinner from the old iron pot. She wanted the meal over and the house tidied before the women got there to cut out the quilt scraps.

"How many ladies are coming this afternoon?" Nancy asked as they sat down to eat.

"Eight or ten, maybe," Mammy said as she served Nancy's plate with a large helping of boiled ham and Smoky Mountain greens. She dipped out a cornmeal dumpling which she added to the rest, then began to pour the hot potlikker into their cups.

Nancy looked thoughtful. Eight or ten weren't very many. She'd have to get other names besides. Maybe she could get off to go down to the crossroads. There were always people there, come to buy things at the store. She began to eat, hungry as a bear after her long trek over the mountains, and never had a boiled dinner tasted better. She wondered if she should tell Mammy about the visit to Uncle Badger's cave, and about the petition. She wondered if it would be a good time to ask to go down to the store to get names. No, it wouldn't, she decided as she took a drink of the hot potlikker. Mammy would be sure to say she might be needed to help out with the quilt. She would be sure to say "no." Better wait until the ladies were here and the work was going forward.

When the meal was over and the dishes washed, Mammy and Nancy sat down to wait for the visitors. The clock hand moved slowly around. Mammy got up, and moved a chair this way, another one that way. Then she rearranged the quilt scraps that were already piled neatly on the bed. She got out her paper quilt patterns, each one rolled and tied, and laid them out in a row beside the quilt scraps. It was one o'clock, then it was two. Why didn't the ladies come? Nancy's spirits began to sink. She had a feeling there would be no names on her paper that day.

"We could begin the cutting ourselves," Mammy fretted, "if only the pattern had been chosen. But I'd hate to take it onto myself to decide which one should be used."

At last there came a light knock on the door. Mammy rushed to open it. Bluett MacMurray was there. She had come to say that her mammy couldn't be at the quilting bee. She was practicing to play for the jitterbug contest.

"She said she knew there would be plenty to cut out the scraps without her," Bluett explained.

After Bluett came Dora. "Aunt Lizzie's got to play the jewsharp for the boogiewoogie band. She knew there would be no lack of hands to do the cutting," she explained.

Then Ella came, bringing a similar excuse from Cousin Letty, followed by Rowena with word from Aunt Rhoda. Each of the ladies had taken it for granted that the others would be there.

"Well!" Mammy put her hands on her hips. "A fine howdy-do!" Then she turned and looked speculatively at the group of little girls. They glanced at one another uneasily. A sudden silence fell.

"Well, girls, it looks like you're elected," Mammy said.

"But—but Mammy," wailed Nancy. "The pattern hasn't been decided on."

"No, it hasn't," her friends exclaimed hopefully. "The pattern hasn't been chosen. We can't cut the quilt if the pattern hasn't been chosen."

"If the women are not a-mind to come, they've got no right to find fault with what we choose," Mammy replied. "I reckon you girls are old enough to know what's pretty. What's your favorite quilt pattern, now?"

The girls all began to answer at once.

"Mine's the Double Wedding Ring," Rowena began enthusiastically. "When Sister got married, we made her a real pretty one."

"Mine's the Kentucky Blazing Star."

"I like the Texas Rattlesnake design!"

"The Irish Chain!" Ella exclaimed. "Our folks brought that one over from Ireland in the old days."

"Wait, wait!" Mammy cried. "We have to think of something fitten. It's for the President, remember. Maybe it ought to have a remembrance of the mountains in it."

"If we give him a rattlesnake design, he might take it we mean he's a snake," Dora tittered.

"No, that's not fitten," Rowena said. "And I reckon the Double Wedding Ring isn't either. The President is not a-getting married."

"How about a Log Cabin Quilt?" Rowena asked. "There's lots of log cabins through the hills."

"Or the zigzag rail fence design," Nancy pointed to one of the patterns on Mammy's bed. "That's the way we make our fences up here."

"We could make the Scotch Thistle design with the Irish Chain all around it," Ella suggested. "That could stand for all the Scotch-Irish here in the mountains. A chance of people up here are Scotch-Irish. Aunt Hettie's got a quilt like that. It's pretty as a picture."

"That's an idea," Mammy said thoughtfully. "Here's the pattern for it." She took one of the patterns from the bed and unrolled it. "But then there are lots of folks, like the Grubers, that came over from Germany. Remember that tulip design that Granny always makes? Her own granny took that from a picture on an old wedding chest her folks brought down the river Rhine, across the ocean, and then down through the mountains of Pennsylvania. Looks like it wouldn't be fair to have the Scotch-Irish remembered and not the Germans."

"No, that wouldn't be fair," the girls agreed.

"I think the Delectable Mountains is the prettiest pattern of all," Bluett said.

"The Delectable Mountains—what's that?" the others exclaimed.

"Why, it's made of peaks, like the mountains. The whole quilt is full of peaks."

"But what does it mean, that 'delectable'?"

"It means delightful and pleasant," Mammy spoke up. "It's an old design. I've known it since I was a girl. There's a book called *The Pilgrim's Progress* that speaks of the Delectable Mountains. It's a religious book they used to read a lot in the old days. It tells of a man that struggles through sloughs of troubles until at last he reaches the Delectable Mountains where it's cool and green—a pleasant resting place on a hard journey. The old folks thought a lot of that design. I reckon it made them think of their own hard journey across the ocean, traipsing a-foot or in slow oxcarts through the wilderness, beset by savages, then at last finding a home here among the green hills."

Mammy held out a quilt square sewn with pointed pieces. "Here's a sample of it I made when I was a young'un."

"Oh, that's the best design of all!" Nancy exclaimed.

"Yes, 'tis. The Delectable Mountains!" the others agreed. "We'll make that one."

"Then gather round the bed, girls. Each take a section of the pattern and choose the scraps you like best," Mammy said.

What a chattering there was as the girls picked out this or that piece of cloth from the bed!

"Here's a piece of that pretty pink dress your sister was married in!"

"I'll take this. It's something left from Mary Anne Gruber's flowered percale."

"Oh, here's a scrap of Uncle Rufus' Sunday shirt!"

The girls sat down together on the big braided rug, cut the

pieces from the scraps of cloth they had chosen, and began to fit them together like pieces of a puzzle.

"When people just poke some cloth at you and say, 'Sew this!' it's no fun to make a quilt," Dora said. "It's different when you can decide on the pattern and choose everything yourself."

"Yes, it is," Nancy agreed. "It's fun when you can pick the pattern and put the colors together the way you want them."

All afternoon the girls sat sewing until the valleys began to fill up with shadows and it was time to go home.

"Tomorrow afternoon we'll all meet at Aunt Rhoda's house," Mammy told them as they were taking their leave. "She's got a quilting frame. Sew all the rest of the pieces together at home and have them all ready to go onto the frame. But your mammies will have to do most of the quilting. It's very particular work—fine stitching. You tell 'em they've got to be there next time."

"We'll tell 'em," the girls called as they walked along the path to the gate.

Yes, quilt-making was fun after all, Nancy decided as she watched her friends disappear. But nothing was as much fun as dancing. Too bad she hadn't got any names on the paper. But no use mourning over what couldn't be helped. Tomorrow she would find time to go to the store, and in the afternoon surely all the women would be at Aunt Rhoda's to do the quilting.

But on the following morning Nancy was busy every minute. There were all the chores to be done—both her own and Fern's and that tiresome, everlasting job of hauling up water. And after dinner when it was time to set off for Aunt Rhoda's, Mammy said, "You run along and get started sewing the parts of the quilt together. I'll be along just as soon as I wash up the dishes."

Nancy set off. A little way along the trail where a great rock ledge overhung the road she started suddenly. A fierce growl sounded. She looked up, her eyes wide with fright. Then she leaped away, screaming. The noise was like the one in the hollow tree when Jodey had jabbed the bear. Then a shock of tousled hair appeared over the ledge followed by a freckled face. It was Jodey, grinning at her impishly.

"Oh, you!" Nancy exclaimed angrily. "I might have known it. You've fooled me so many times, like as not I wouldn't run if a varmint took after me. I'd be sure it was you."

Jodey laughed and swung himself down onto the path. "How are you coming with the paper?" he asked.

Nancy explained to him what had happened the day before. "Maybe you'd better take it and go down to the store with it."

"Pappy's sent me to borrow Uncle Joe's mule. I've got to get right back home and plow up some new ground," Jodey said.

"Well, anyway, I'll get the names of all the ladies that are coming to do the quilting," said Nancy hopefully.

They were coming near Aunt Rhoda's house. Nancy looked around uneasily. "Where's that old spotted sow?" Her eyes went darting quickly among the pink flowering laurel bushes in the yard.

"She's there," Jodey pointed toward the barn lot. "Shut up safe in her pen."

In the cabin the big quilting frame was already hanging from its four hooks in the ceiling. All the little girls were seated, each sewing her part of the quilt to that of another.

Nancy looked around as she entered. Not one of the women was present, with the exception of Aunt Rhoda herself. "Aren't your mammies coming?" she cried in alarm.

"Mine's coming," Bluett said. "She was real put out when she found out nobody showed up to help out yesterday. She'll be here for sure, as soon as she washes up the dinner dishes. They'll all be here."

"Come on in, Jodey," Aunt Rhoda cried, spying him in the door. "Get yourself a needle. The best tailors are men!"

"No sirree!" Jodey shook his head. "You don't rope me into no women's work. Mountain men ain't tailors. I only came to borrow a mule."

"Uncle Joe's out there in the barn lot," Aunt Rhoda said. "He'll let you have one."

"Have a big time, girls," Jodey said as he turned to go.

"Huh! We're not expecting no excitement," Dora said.

"You never can tell, girls; you never can tell!" Jodey gave them a sly wink.

A puzzled glance passed between Dora and Nancy. Now what did he mean by that? What was that Jodey up to now?

Nancy sat down with the others and began to sew her part of the quilt to one end of Dora's, while Dora stitched the other end of her work to Rowena's piece.

"It's about time those women were a-coming." Aunt Rhoda looked at the clock on the mantelpiece. "It's going on two."

Nancy began to feel uneasy. Maybe it would be like yesterday and the women wouldn't come.

As the girls stitched on and on they began to talk about the prize offered for the dance contest.

"You know what I thought of?" Bluett said.

"No, what?"

"A watermelon."

"But that's green. The verse said heavy as lead and colored red."

"It's red inside, a watermelon is. Maybe the verse meant the inside part was red."

"Oh, but there's another hint out now," Rowena said. "They've made up another verse." She began to recite:

> It rumbles and it bumbles,
> It's stronger than a mule.
> It saves the young'uns time to play,
> And time to go to school!

"Gracious sakes!" The girls looked blank. "It can't be any watermelon then. A watermelon doesn't rumble and bumble."

"I know!" Ella cried. "I'll bet you a pretty it's a water-wheel churn!"

The others looked at her, needles poised. "A water-wheel churn—what's that?"

"There was a man up in Squirrel Cove invented one. It's an earthenware churn, real heavy, like it says in the verse. There's a paddle wheel inside it. You put your cream in, take it to the brook where there's a wheel turned by the water. You fasten the paddle wheel to the water wheel. And there it goes, rumbling and bumbling. It makes the butter come all by itself. The young'uns don't have to sit churning all morning long, they can go out and play. Now doesn't that verse fit that churn exactly?"

"But is it colored red?"

"It can't be stronger than a mule!"

There was a babble of talk all at once.

"Hush!" Nancy suddenly hissed. She put one hand to her ear as if listening to something outside.

The girls were quiet, listening. There was no sound except the chirping of birds in the laurel bushes. "What did you hear?"

"I declare, it sounded mighty like a screech owl," Nancy replied in a puzzled voice.

"Whoever heard of a screech owl hollering in the middle of the afternoon?" said Aunt Rhoda. "A screech owl's a night bird. It couldn't have been that!"

Nobody thought of an explanation for the noise and the girls went on with their work. The various parts of the quilt were at last sewed together and they held it up.

"It's lovely!" Aunt Rhoda exclaimed. "As pretty a quilt top as I ever saw. They're delectable mountains, sure enough. It's ready now to put the lining on and the padding in. Then we can get it onto the frame. Now why don't those women come on? All ready to do the quilting and they're not here yet."

Nancy had a sinking feeling. The afternoon was wearing away. Something had happened. She was sure of it. Another day would pass and there were no names on her paper.

"Is this the stuff for the lining?" Aunt Rhoda unfolded the yellow cloth that Dora had given to Nancy. "My stars!—Why girls, this must be the stuff Great-aunt Lizzie wove for her wedding dress. They said it was yellow linen made from flax her pa raised on the place and dyed with yellow sassafras blooms picked on the hillsides."

The girls looked up. Great-aunt Lizzie with a face like a shriveled autumn leaf—had she ever been young and in love?

"But—but Aunt Lizzie never married!" Dora exclaimed in astonishment.

"No, she was never married. The MacMurray's hogs put an end to that."

The girls stared, perplexed. A funny thing that hogs could put an end to a marriage.

"You see, they were to be married in June," Aunt Rhoda began to explain. "Lizzie's beau, Al Calloway, planted a vegetable garden so's he and his bride would have something to eat during the summer and something to put up for the winter. There weren't any stores to run to in those days. But one morning the hogs got in and rooted up the garden. Al was so mad he got his shotgun and killed those hogs, every one of them. That left the MacMurrays with no meat for the next winter and they were mad a sight about that. They hid along the trail one night and shot Al dead. That put an end to the wedding for sure.

"And it started a feud between the two families, for Al's brothers began shooting off the MacMurrays out of revenge and the MacMurrays in their turn began to shoot off Al's brothers. Pretty soon nigh every family in the mountains had taken one side or the other and no man could walk the mountain trails without fear of a shot from behind every tree or rock. It got so—"

"Aunt Rhoda, wait—" Ella suddenly exclaimed. She held up a finger for quiet.

Aunt Rhoda and the girls looked at her in surprise. "What's the matter?" they inquired after a long pause.

"Didn't you hear that sound?"

The girls shook their heads. "What was it like?"

"It sounded something like the night wind blowing up from the valley. You know how it mourns sometimes, real lonesome-like. But still, it wasn't the wind. It was something else."

They all sat quiet, listening. There was only the sound of a dog barking on some distant ridge.

"I didn't hear anything." Aunt Rhoda looked out the window.

The bushes and trees stood motionless. "There's no wind at all. Ella, you and Nancy have got bats in your belfries, that's what." She lifted the quilt top and put it on the yellow cloth, over a padding of soft white wool. Then the girls stood around it and lifted it by the four sides. They placed it carefully on the quilting frame.

"I don't believe your mammies are coming at all." Aunt Rhoda fastened the long strips of wood that held the quilt tightly on the frame. "Maybe I'd better try to show you girls how to do this quilting."

"Oh! do, Aunt Rhoda! We can learn!" chorused the girls. They gathered around as Aunt Rhoda sat down beside the frame and began to push her needle in and out, making a scalloped design as she went. Then with their own needles they began to follow her example. It wasn't hard to do and the needles went flashing in and out.

Outside, the shadows of the mountains stretched themselves longer and longer, and shaded into deep violet. Uncle Joe came home from the fields. They could hear him drawing water. The chains went rattling through the pulley as the bucket fell back into the well.

Suddenly Rowena cried, "Pappy, be quiet! Listen—a strange noise. I heard it!"

Uncle Joe held the bucket. They all paused, listening. There was nothing except the distant clanking of cowbells as the cows wound their way homeward over the hills.

"What did it sound like?" the girls asked, full of curiosity.

"It was a wailing sound. I declare I thought I heard a wailing way off yonder. It was like—well, maybe like a whippoorwill call."

"Shucks, young'un," said Aunt Rhoda. "What's the matter with you? A whippoorwill wouldn't be calling at this hour. They come out only after night begins to fall."

"But I heard something queer. I sure did!" Rowena insisted. And Nancy and Ella declared just as positively that they had heard something, too. What could it be—that mysterious noise? The girls shook their heads in perplexity, then went on with the quilting.

"I declare you girls are going loony," Aunt Rhoda laughed. "A-hearing things that aren't there!"

"Won't you sing us a song, Aunt Rhoda, to while away the

time?" asked Nancy. "Sing us the ballad of the 'Farmer's Curst Wife'."

"Oh that one!" laughed Aunt Rhoda. She took the dulcimer down from the wall and sat down with it across her lap. She struck a few tinkling chords and began:

> There was an old farmer lived under a hill,
> He had a little farm and on it did dwell.
> The devil came to him one day at the plow,
> Said, "One of your family I have to have now!"

"Twice fa la," the little girls joined in singing the chorus. "Fa lilly, fa lay, rio!"

And then Aunt Rhoda went on to sing of the farmer's quarrelsome old wife who was caught by the devil, stuffed into his sack, and carried off to the place down below. But even down there the old wife kicked up jack and no one could abide her.

"The poor old farmer, he peeped through the crack," sang Aunt Rhoda stroking away on the dulcimer.

> And saw the devil a-wagging her back.
> The poor old man, he took to his bed,
> She upped with the butter stick and paddled his head!.
> And now you see what a woman can do—
> She can outdo the devil and her old man, too!

"Twice fa la," the girls shouted until the rafters rang, "Fa lilly, fa lay, rio!"

They had hardly finished when they became aware of a noise. This time everyone heard it, even Aunt Rhoda. From the direction of the road yells and shrieks were coming nearer by the second.

"There, you see, we *have* been hearing something!" Rowena cried.

They all ran to the door.

"Help, help!" Along the road a crowd of women came running, shrieking as they ran. In the forefront came Jodey, speeding like the wind.

"There's Mammy!" cried Nancy, amazed.

"Aunt Lizzie—all of 'em!" Dora exclaimed.

"What's ailing 'em?" wondered Ella.

The girls stood astonished at the sight of Jodey and their mothers rushing toward them, their dresses flying, their hair falling down about their ears.

"Looks like they've gone clean crazy!" exclaimed Aunt Rhoda. "Here they come. Stand back, girls, you'll be trampled."

The girls jumped away from the door, and only just in time. Jodey and the shrieking women rushed through in a mob. They climbed up on chairs, leaped on the bed, clung to the window ledges. On their heels, snorting fiercely, came Aunt Rhoda's spotted sow.

In a panic, the girls climbed on the table. "Help, help, Uncle Joe!"

"What's a-going on here?" Uncle Joe looked in, astonished. "Sounds like judgment day—" He broke off as he caught sight of the sow charging around the room.

"Why, you old she-witch!" He looked about for a weapon to drive out the invading beast. Seeing nothing else, he seized the side rail from the bed where the women were standing.

Crash! The mattress fell to the floor. With it fell the women and Jodey in a jumble.

Uncle Joe went after the angry sow and chased her from the room. He drove her back to her pen.

On the fallen bed, the women sat dazed, not yet able to understand what had happened. Finally they began to scramble up. The girls ventured down from the table top. Nancy and the other women came down from chairs and window ledges.

Finally Aunt Rhoda gathered her wits to ask, "What happened? Where were you all afternoon?"

"Where were we!" cried Aunt Lizzie. "Where but hanging up a tree!"

"Up a tree!" exclaimed Aunt Rhoda and the girls.

"With that mean old sow down below, looking up at us, charging around, snorting, ready to chew up the first one that ventured down."

"We were walking along the road as peaceful as you please," said Aunt Hettie. "And here she came a-tearing outen the bushes. We ran for a tree—"

"And there we stayed," broke in Mrs. MacMurray, "a-clinging to the branches. Every now and then we'd holler to see if we couldn't make you hear us. But ne'er a soul came near us. Couldn't ye hear us hollering?"

"Every now and then the girls heard something," Aunt Rhoda confessed. "But they thought it was screech owls."

"Screech owls!"

The girls couldn't help giggling.

"After a while the old beast walked off," said Aunt Lizzie. "We thought she'd gone away so we came down from the tree. But she was only hiding in the bushes."

"Oh my lands!" interrupted Mrs. MacMurray. "And there's

the quilting to do! Well, I'm just too raddled to do any quilting tonight."

"Start on that quilting now, after spending the afternoon hanging up a tree!" cried Cousin Letty. "I should say not. I'll be lucky to be able to stagger on back home."

This seemed to be the feeling of all the ladies. Aunt Rhoda hurried to put on a pot of sassafras tea to revive them but they wouldn't wait to drink it.

"It's way past time to start supper," Granny Gruber said. "We've got to get off right away."

Nancy thought of the paper to be signed. She took it out of her pocket and began to explain it, but the women wouldn't stop to listen. They hurried off, calling to the girls to come along.

Uncle Joe came in and replaced the side rail on the bed. "Now how do you reckon that sow got outen her pen?" he remarked as he put the slats back in place and laid the feather bed upon them. "I was extra careful to fasten her door because I didn't want her a-charging at the women when they came. But when I went out a while ago, there the door was, wide open."

Nancy and Dora glanced at each other, then at Jodey who was standing beside the fireplace. They had an idea how that door got open.

The girls began to take their leave. "We've done this quilt so far all by ourselves," Rowena said. "It would be fun to finish it. Then maybe we could walk upon the platform at the big doin's and give it to the President with our own hands."

"Oh, that would be wonderful!" the others exclaimed. "Why can't we do it?"

"No reason why you can't," Aunt Rhoda said. "The quilt is

more than half done already. Come back tomorrow as early as you can. We've got two more days before the doin's. In that time you could finish it."

"That's what we'll do. We'll be here early. We'll finish the quilt all by ourselves!" the girls cried enthusiastically. They said good-by to Aunt Rhoda and Uncle Joe and went hurrying along the trail toward their houses.

Nancy didn't feel as happy as the rest. She looked hard at Jodey who was walking with her and Dora. "How did that old sow get outen her pen?" she demanded. "You had something to do with it, I know you did."

"Well," Jodey grinned in a shamefaced way. "I just thought I'd have a little fun. I thought I'd let the sow out and see her chase the women over the fence. I meant to drive her off right away and let them go on into the house to their quilting. But the old critter got the drop on *me.* I thought to open the door and then jump on the fence outen her way. But I didn't have time. She was quick as lightning—outen that door and after me before I could turn around. She chased me outen the yard and way down the road. At last, I jumped for a tree limb and swung myself up. And there I sat with that sow down below. Everybody that came along, she jumped 'em and chased 'em up a tree. And there we were all afternoon with that critter charging and snorting around the foot of the tree. I didn't get home with the mule and Pappy's a-going to be mad."

"Serves you right!" Dora exclaimed.

"A great help you are," Nancy said. "Tomorrow you'll be plowing and maybe the next day, and I'll be stuck with that quilting job. And whenever are we going to get that paper signed?"

## 5. Right Outen the Sky

It was the afternoon of the big doin's. Pappy was at the barn hitching the horse to the jolt-wagon while in the house the womenfolk primped and prettied. In her little attic room Nancy slipped her new pink dress over her head. It was a present from her big brother, Zach, who was earning cash money working on the dam. She whirled herself about to see the skirt umbrella outward. What a fine dress for dancing! She couldn't resist knocking out a few lively clogs.

"Hey you!" came a yell from Fern downstairs. "You're knocking the dust outen the ceiling!"

Nancy stopped dancing. She sighed, remembering that she would have no chance to dance at the doin's but would have to sit watching the others. The petition was there on the chest. She hadn't had a moment to take it around, and neither had Jodey. She'd been able to get the names of those in the house, Mammy and Pappy, and those nearby, Great-aunt Lizzie, Aunt Rhoda, and Uncle Joe—that was all. It made only five names, not nearly enough. To be in the contest Nancy and Jodey would have to get twenty-five more. But it was too late now, no use to think about it.

"Well, anyway, the quilt is finished," Nancy comforted herself. The Delectable Mountains—a beautiful job! Both Mammy and Aunt Rhoda said so. She and the other girls had done it, every stitch, with their own hands. And now they were going to be allowed to march up onto the stage and give it to the President. And I'm the one who's going to hand it to him! Nancy thought. Bluett would make a little speech, and after that, Nancy would step forward and put the quilt in the President's hands. Thinking of it made her feel proud but it didn't entirely lift that lump of disappointment on her chest.

"Hurry up!" Mammy called to her. "I promised to get there an hour early to help make the lemonade. We've a mighty heap of lemons to squeeze out."

"An hour early." The words gave Nancy an idea. Why not take the paper along? During that hour, when the ladies were squeezing lemons, she could get people to sign their names. Then at the last moment she could hand it up to Grandpa Gruber. Yes, it was a grand idea! She flew around, combing her hair, pulling on the pink socks Zach had sent her along with the dress, polishing her shoes. She and Jodey might be in that contest after all!

"Let's go!" came a shout from outside. Nancy looked out the window. In front of the house was the jolt-wagon piled high with hay. Aunt Lizzie and Dora, who were going with them, were already seated on it. Pappy was on the bench and Mammy and Fern were climbing up.

Nancy grabbed the paper from the top of the chest, hurried down the ladder, and ran to the wagon. She climbed up.

"Get along there!" Pappy cracked his whip. The horse started at a lively trot. It was a beautiful afternoon. There had been rain in the morning and the foliage was washed and shining. The air was sparkling, and the waves and rows of blue ranges that usually looked so pale and distant stood out sharp and clear with white clouds floating high above.

"A fine day for a speaking!" Pappy exclaimed. Then he burst out singing.

> Chickens crowing on Sourwood Mountain!

Everybody joined in.

> Hi, ho, diddle dum day!
> Get your dogs and we'll go hunting,
> Hi, ho, diddle dum day!

Even the horse seemed to know it was a special day. He picked up his heels and trotted with fine spirit. At this rate they'd be there in no time, Nancy thought happily and fingered the petition lying in her lap.

> My true love lives up the river
> Hi, ho, diddle dum day!
> A few more jumps and I'll be wiv'er,
> Hi, ho, diddle dum day!

At the branch road that led in from the mill they overtook the MacMurrays, trudging along on foot. Pappy hauled back on the reins.

"Hey there, what's happened to that car of yours?" he called out.

"The doggone jalopy went cranky on me," Mr. MacMurray exclaimed. "Couldn't get the thing started to save my soul. Everybody cranked her, but there she sat—wouldn't move."

"Climb up with us," Pappy invited. "The more, the merrier!"

Mr. MacMurray heaved himself thankfully onto the back of the wagon. He hauled up Mrs. MacMurray, while Bluett and Daniel scrambled up over the wheel. Pappy flicked the reins and they were off. Nancy noticed uneasily that the horse didn't go nearly so fast now. But the jogging pace didn't seem to trouble anybody.

Pappy raised another tune.

> I used to have an old gray horse,
> He weighted ten thousand pounds.
> Every tooth he had in his head
> Was eighteen inches around.

Everybody shouted the chorus.

> I'm a-going down to town!
> I'm a-going down to town,
> I'm a-going down to Asheville town
> To carry my tobacco down!

They jogged along beneath the shadow of Thunderhead Mountain that towered up beside the road. Glancing upward, Nancy caught sight of three people high on a trail that zigzagged down the shaggy slope. I'll not mention *them,* she said to herself. We've load enough already. Then she looked sharper. Something about the smallest one made her think of Jodey. Could it be Jodey and his mammy and pappy stumping down the path?

She peered and peered. Yes it was, for sure and certain. She jog-gled Pappy's arm and pointed.

Pappy looked up. "Well, for the land sakes! Now what in blazes—that's your Uncle Matt and Aunt Sallie Calloway and there's Jodey." He stopped the horse and waited. When they were within hollering distance, he cupped his hands and shouted.

"What you doing coming over the mountain? What happened to that horse of yours?"

"Went lame," Uncle Matt shouted back. He hurried down the path with Aunt Sallie and Jodey at his heels. On they came, zig-zagging down the steep mountainside. When they were closer, Uncle Matt began to explain. "The horse got a stone jammed under his shoe yesterday. Didn't know it until I went out to hitch up. His foot was so sore he could hardly hobble. So we had to set off walking."

"We thought we'd make better time if we took a short cut over the mountain," Aunt Sallie added. "But I don't think it helped much. Looks like we're going to get there after the doin's are half over."

"Want to get up and ride with us?" Pappy invited. "Though I reckon you wouldn't be going so very much faster."

"Don't care if we do," Aunt Sallie sighed with relief as she climbed aboard. "That mountain has pretty near winded me."

Jodey found a place near Nancy. "How about the petition?" he whispered. "Did you get all the names?"

"No, I didn't." Nancy shook her head as the horse leaned for-ward in the traces to get the wagon going. "I've got only five names. It was the best I could do."

Jodey looked glum. "And I've had never a moment the whole

week. Pappy's had me plowing until after sundown every day."

"I'm hoping we'll get there early," Nancy whispered. "We got an early start because Mammy wanted to help make the lemonade. While she squeezes lemons, you and I could rush around and get the rest of the names on our petition. We could hand it up to Grandpa Gruber at the last minute."

"Why, sure we could!" Jodey's eyes lit with enthusiasm. "We'll get into that contest as sure as shooting."

"But the horse is going so slow." Nancy frowned anxiously. "We started out trotting like going to a house afire. But Pappy's picked up the MacMurrays and now you all. I don't begrudge anybody a ride, you least of all, but I sure do hate to see the horse slow down so. Just look—he's only shambling along."

"Maybe if we don't pick up anybody else, not *anybody*, we'll get there yet, with enough time to get folks to sign their names. Look down the road. See anybody up ahead?"

Nancy, who was sitting higher on the hay, peered forward. She groaned. "Yes, I do—a man carrying a fiddle by the neck. It's Uncle Rufus. Ella's tagging beside him. And there's Aunt Hettie straggling way behind. Now what can have happened that they're afoot? We'll have to pick *them* up for sure!" Nancy's hopes sank.

The wagon jolted on. When it drew abreast of Aunt Hettie, Pappy stopped the horse. "Hey, what you doing afoot?" he howled at the top of his voice.

"What say?" Auntie put a hand behind her ear.

Pappy leaned closer. "I say, what you doing afoot? Where's that old plug mule of yours?"

"Why, folks," Auntie looked up at the crowd in the wagon. Her voice was full of astonishment. "That mule began to talk this morning. Yes, he did. He talked. We didn't dare drive him."

Everybody began to exclaim, "He talked? The mule?"

"That's what they told me. They said the mule talked. What he said I don't know. Maybe he said he didn't want to go to the doin's. Maybe he said he woudn't haul us. Anyway here we are afoot and I'm wore plumb down to a frazzle." Aunt Hettie mopped her perspiring face.

People in the wagon looked at each other.

"Maybe the mule was against building the dam in the first place," Jodey shouted. "Like Uncle Badger."

"Maybe so," agreed Aunt Hettie.

"Looks like all the critters are against it, the way they've laid down on the job this morning," Mr. MacMurray said. "And the automobiles, too. Don't know as I blame them."

"Well, Auntie, crawl up with us." Pappy and Mr. MacMurray got down and hoisted her aboard. "We'll see what Uncle Rufus has to say about this business."

"Mules didn't talk in my day." Aunt Hettie shook her head as she sank down in the hay. "No, they didn't. Such progress—it takes a body by surprise. I never even heard tell of a mule's talking in my time, or any other critter. I declare things are getting 'way beyond me."

The horse stirred himself to a lagging trot and they overtook Uncle Rufus and Ella. Pappy pulled on the reins and called out, "Say, what's all this I hear about your mule? Aunt Hettie said he talked this morning."

"No, no, no!" said Uncle Rufus crossly. "I didn't say he talked. I said he baulked. Yes, that's what he did, he baulked on me, the ornery critter. Couldn't make him go nohow. I tried everything. Even built a fire under him."

"Built a fire under him!" cried the friends in the wagon. "And that didn't make him go?"

"He only walked a few steps forward and left the fire under the wagon. Burnt it clean up."

"Well, I swan! Gollies!" everybody exclaimed in sympathy.

"Get up with us, you two," Pappy invited. "Always room for a few more."

"We thank you kindly." Uncle Rufus laid his fiddle on the hay, gave Ella a boost, then climbed up himself.

Nancy looked at Jodey. With this load it would be a wonder if the horse could manage a walk. She made room for Ella beside her and the others moved over for Uncle Rufus. The wagon began to creak on down the trail.

"I'm afraid I won't get there in time to help make the lemonade," Mammy said a little anxiously. Then she added in a more cheerful tone, "But no matter. If I don't, there'll be others to do it without me."

"There won't be others to get the names on our petition." Nancy turned a dismayed face to Jodey. The horse had slowed to a plodding walk.

"And look ahead." Jodey got to his knees. "Up the road a piece, there's somebody else hobbling along."

"Oh, my!" Fern began to worry too. "If this keeps up we'll not get there in time for the dance contest. Whoever can that be?" She stared toward the distant figure.

They had turned onto the wide road that led through the valley. The man ahead was limping along the side path, stopping now and then as if to rest. As they came nearer, they recognized Uncle Badger. His banjo was slung across his back and he was hobbling along, his face wrinkled into lines of pain.

As they came abreast of him, Mammy called out, "Whatever's the matter with you, Uncle Badger?"

"Went and got me a pair of store-bought shoes for the big doin's," Uncle Badger said. "They're murdering my feet. Wore a blister on my heel and skinned my big toe. If I didn't have to play in the boogiewoogie band I'd sure-to-Betsy sit down right here and not go another step!"

"Climb up with us, Uncle Badger. Don't know when we'll get there, but we'll make it sometime or other."

"Sure do thank you." Uncle Badger mounted over the wagon wheel and sat down with Nancy and Jodey. "Wouldn't take a pretty for this ride!" He took off his shoes and groaned with relief. Then he looked at his young companions. "What's the matter with you, young'uns, your shoes pinching, too?"

"We didn't get time to go around with the petition," Nancy said, "and we're still a-hankering to be in that contest."

"Jeepers creepers, you've got half of Razorback Ridge right here in the wagon. Pass it around now."

Nancy brought out the paper. Uncle Badger explained it to the passengers.

"Why sure, we'll sign it," Uncle Rufus exclaimed. "I'd ruther see Nancy and Jodey dance than eat sugar candy!"

The paper was handed from one to the other. But after all had signed there were still only twelve names. Uncle Badger looked at them and scratched his head.

"It does look discouraging, for a fact. But perk up, child, sometimes opportunity drops right outen the sky. Be ready to grab it. If you cloud yourself over with gloom, you won't see it if it falls."

His advice didn't make Nancy feel any more hopeful. She

didn't have faith that opportunity would fall from the sky. But she wanted to please Uncle Badger so she put on a cheerful face. Somehow it made her *feel* more cheerful.

The horse was going so slowly now that it seemed to Nancy the wagon wheels were scarcely turning, yet she knew they were, for up ahead the big dam was looming larger and larger.

"What a master pile of concrete!" Jodey stared up at it.

"And it cost a master pile of money, I can tell you!" Mr. Mac-Murray frowned as he peered upward. "And what the good of it is, I don't know."

"It's a monster thing—as big as the mountain behind Grandpa Gruber's house," Ella said.

Beneath some tall trees at the foot of the dam an outdoor stage had been built. Bright-colored bunting was draped around it and flags were flying gaily above it.

"What a slew of folks!" Dora stared. Throngs of people were seated about the stage on homemade benches, hundreds more stood around the edges. They filled the field around about, like a lake that had overflowed its banks.

On the stage sat many important-looking people.

"Looky!" Nancy nudged Jodey. "There's the President. He's just like his pictures."

"Well, I swan, he sure is!"

Pappy drove his horse under some pine trees on the edge of the grounds and his passengers began to scramble up from the hay.

"Lawsy me, we're late, sure enough!" Aunt Lizzie stood up and peered toward the stage. "Looky, Grandpa Gruber is up making a speech!" She took her jew's-harp out of her pocket and began to twang it nervously.

"Too late to start practicing now!" Uncle Badger slung his banjo off his back. "Jeepers! I hope we're not too late to play in the boogiewoogie band. Where's it at, I wonder?" He gazed anxiously about.

"We've got to find Rowena. She's got the quilt," Dora said to Nancy.

"It would be awful if we didn't find her," Bluett cried. "Suppose they call out our names to come up and give the President the quilt and we haven't got any quilt!"

"Where are the jitterbugs?" Mr. MacMurray peered around with a worried look.

"There they are!" Fern had caught sight of Mary Anne beckoning them frantically from up front near the band. "Come on!"

she grabbed Daniel's hand and they climbed hurriedly over the wagon wheel.

"Come on, Pa, you and Ma follow us!" Daniel called back as he and Fern began to push through the mob.

Everybody was climbing out of the wagon. The four girls craned their necks, looking for Rowena and the quilt.

There's no time to get any more names, Nancy thought. Even if we had the petition all signed, it would be too late. Grandpa Gruber is already up making a speech. We couldn't give it to him. No chance for Jodey and me now—our last, our very last chance is gone!

"There's Rowena!" Ella exclaimed. "Up front near the jitter-bugs. She's saved us some seats. Come on!" She and Bluett and Dora leaped from the back of the wagon. Nancy followed them.

"Got your feet limbered up for that contest?" Jodey grinned as he leaped down beside her.

"Huh!" retorted Nancy. "What's the use to think of that now?"

"You remember what Uncle Badger said a while back?" Jodey gave her a sly wink. "You never can tell!" Then he was away, running through the crowd.

"What do you mean? Hey, wait—" Nancy called out. But Jodey didn't stop. She saw him catch up with Uncle Badger, say a few words, then dart on. After that she lost sight of him. What kind of mischief was he up to, that Jodey? But there was no time to worry about it now.

She was hurrying after Bluett and the other girls through crowds of people when she felt a hand on her shoulder. She looked up.

"Brother Zach!" Her big brother stood smiling down at her, his blue eyes bright and twinkling. She gave him a delighted hug.

"Golly, you look important!" She gazed admiringly on his new suit and handsome straw hat.

"I am important, about as important as the President," Zach winked at her. "I'm the fellow that built the dam—with a lot of other mountain goats. They did a little something, too. We're pretty proud of it, all joking aside. How do you like it?" he glanced up at the towering structure that held back so much water.

"Mighty big. But what's the good of it, that's what I want to know. A great big monstrous thing like that—what's it fur?"

"You'll find out. The President is a-going to tell you." Then he held her off at arm's length and looked her over. "You look pretty swell yourself, Sis."

"It's the new dress you sent me. It's the purtiest one I ever had. I thank you for it, Zach."

"You're going to look purty as a picture up there dancing in that contest. Just wait until you see the prize. We fellows took up a collection and raised a pile of money. We bought something fine. It's something you'll like, Sis. Make those little feet fly when you get up there on that stage. Do your darndest, you hear!" He gave her a hug and hurried away.

Do her darndest—and not even a chance to try! Nancy's heart felt sick—but only for a moment. There was no time to mope. She had to find Rowena and the other girls. They were depending on her to present the quilt. There they were, sitting in a row right at the front. She scurried down the aisle and slid into the seat they had saved for her.

"Gollies, I was afraid you weren't coming." Rowena leaned forward and put the quilt into her hands. She whispered, "In a moment the President is going to make a speech. When he's through, they're going to have the dance contest. After that we march up and give him the quilt."

Nancy nodded. She took the quilt and sat down to wait.

"As I understand it—" Grandpa Gruber was saying, motioning toward the dam, "it works something like the MacMurray's mill. The water turns the wheels, but instead of grinding corn it makes electricity. And now, folks, I don't have to tell you who this is," he nodded toward the President. "We're all honored to hear from the President of the United States."

Everybody clapped as the President stood up.

"My friends," the President began. "We all know that mountain ways are good ways—" A burst of applause made the President pause. When it had quieted down, he went on. "It's good to plow your own land, raise your own food, can your own vegetables, and be ready for the winter. It's good to have your own cow in the barn and your own chickens in the hen house."

"Amen, President!" Grandpa Gruber nodded his head until his white corn-silk beard waggled.

"It's good to help each other the way you do up here, to have cornhuskings and house-raisings—folks getting together to help out a neighbor. It's good to go to church and sing the old hymns. It's good to go hunting together and hear the hound dogs baying on the mountains!"

"Yippee!" came a yell from a tall tree that leaned over the stage.

Nancy looked up. It was Jodey, hanging onto a limb and waving his hat. The tree was full of boys roosting like birds. He'd better hold on, she thought, or he'll be hollering for another reason.

"Yes, mountain ways are good ways," the President con-

tinued. "We wouldn't want to change them. This dam is not going to change them. It will only make them better. It's going to stop the floods that are washing your fields away. It's one of a whole chain of dams that will hold back the water that comes rushing down the slopes every year, carrying your good topsoil away. Pretty soon your fields will be rich again as they were in the old days when the land was new.

"Down the river a little way one of these dams is manufacturing a fine phosphate fertilizer. They're making it so cheaply that all can afford to buy it. It's going to help bring your land back to fertility and the corn will be growing as it did for your grandsires—all the way to the eaves of your homes!"

"Whoopee!" The mountain men threw up their hats.

"There'll be no more hot work for you women, standing over a stove in the summertime canning your fruit and vegetables, no more stirring and stirring in the old brass preserving kettle. With electricity available, you can all club together and buy a freezer with lockers. Then you can pick your fruit and vegetables and put them in it. And there they'll be months later, field-fresh and ready to eat."

"Gee, that would be wonderful!" Dora said to Nancy as the women burst into rounds of applause. "Remember those strawberry preserves?" Then she was struck with a gloomy thought. "But where's the money coming from to buy such things?"

"Oh, I know what you're all thinking," the President seemed to read their minds. "You're asking yourselves where the money is coming from. When this dam gets going there will be jobs for all. Where there's plenty of electricity, factories begin to go up. They're already going up—factories to weave cloth, mills to roll out sheets of aluminum, plants to built aeroplanes. Down the river there's already a big shipbuilding yard. Boats will ply across that lake up there, carrying freight and passengers. You'll be making money from fishing and boating."

The mountain people looked at each other. This was something they hadn't dreamed of.

"Yes, there will be plenty of jobs for all that want to work," the President nodded at them. "There will be jobs for all the boys and girls as soon as they finish school."

Someone tapped Nancy on the back. She turned her head. Fern was sitting behind her, leaning forward. "Didn't I tell you! I'll have a job one of these days and I'll have that modernistic furniture and a satin coverlet, too."

"Some folks say this dam is a handout," the President's face crinkled into a smile. "We think it's an investment—money laid out to make more money. We think you hill folk will make this dam pay for itself a hundred times over—"

"We'll make her pay. Sure as shooting!" Uncle Badger waved his banjo.

"Sure will!" came shouts of agreement.

The President went on. "The things you manufacture up here will be sent out over the whole land to make more business and more jobs for everybody. If you mountain folk do your part, this dam will make the whole country richer and stronger and happier!"

"We'll do it!" came a thundering shout. "Count on us!"

The President sat down with the cheers of the mountain people ringing up to the sky.

And now it was time for the dance contest. Grandpa Gruber stood up and announced it. There was an eager rustling and whispering in the audience. Across the aisle from Nancy the boogiewoogie band began to tune up. She could hear Uncle Rufus' fiddle wailing up and down the scale. Then came plunking notes from Uncle Badger's banjo. It made her think of all the times they had tuned up to play for Jodey and herself. And now to be out of it! She saw the jitterbugs marching up onto the stage. They looked grim and nervous.

And then the band struck up. It was full of fire, but not quite together. Aunt Rhoda, with her tinkling dulcimer, was a little ahead. Mrs. MacMurray followed with the drum, a little behind. The others went their own way—Aunt Lizzie madly plucking the jew's-harp, Mrs. Gruber pounding the piano. Uncle Badger glared around, stomping his foot hard to make the others keep time. Uncle Rufus nodded, scraping away, his fiddle screeching like a cat with its tail caught in the door. My, what a racket!

The dancers went whirling and leaping and stomping. Nancy's eyes popped open to see the miller lift his partner and bounce her into the air. Daniel was whirling Fern like a top. All the young folk were cutting such didoes as the old blue mountains had never looked down on before. The President laughed and clapped, and the crowd shouted with enjoyment. Up in the tree over the stage, Jodey held on with one hand and waved his hat with the other.

Then it was over. The musicians stopped playing and began to mop their faces. Breathing hard, the dancers marched down from the stage. Grandpa Gruber stood up. He thanked the dancers and the band.

"And now the little girls of Razorback Ridge will please come forward," he said. "They've a remembrance for the President, made with their own hands. Meanwhile the judges can retire and decide on who's to have the prize for the best dancing."

The girls looked at each other and stood up. Nancy clutched the quilt. She straightened her pink skirt and fluffed out her hair. Bluett whispered nervously to herself to make sure she hadn't forgotten her speech. Then she led the line up onto the stage. Nancy came at the end, carrying the quilt. They stood in a row in front of the President.

"This quilt was made by the girls of Razorback Ridge," began Bluett and gestured toward the line of girls. "The design was made by our great-great-grandmothers after they reached these hills at the end of a long, hard journey. They called it the Delectable Mountains. We hope you'll rest as thankfully underneath it as they did 'neath the shade of these blue hills!" Bluett pointed toward the surrounding ranges. Then she made a curtsey and stepped back into the line.

Nancy came forward. The President smiled and took the quilt she held out to him. He was about to thank her when there was a sudden crashing in the tree over his head. People in the audience gasped. Someone screamed. Others leaped up.

Nancy looked up. Jodey was tumbling through the branches. He caught on one and fell through another. On the last limb he stuck for a moment. The limb bent almost down to the stage, then it tumbled him off onto the boards. For a moment he sat as if dazed.

Nancy stood, too startled to move. Grandpa Gruber jumped up and bent over Jodey. The judges, who had got up to cast their votes, stood in the aisle, staring. The President exclaimed, "Are you hurt, son?"

Jodey got up. "Let me see . . ." He shuffled one foot. "That's O.K." Then he shuffled the other. "That seems to be all right too." Then he began to shuffle both feet at once.

Uncle Badger's banjo suddenly rang out, playing a merry tune.

"Both feet all right!" Jodey seized Nancy by the arm and broke into a lively buck-and-wing. Without a thought, Nancy began to dance with him. Then she paused, frightened. This wasn't according to their plan, not what they had decided at the schoolhouse. Grandpa Gruber hadn't given them permission to dance! She glanced about. The other girls were marching from the stage. They were taking seats in the row down below. She made a move to follow.

"Hi-yi, foot it, Nancy!" someone in the audience shouted.

"Go it, Jodey and Nancy!" came a roar from the crowd. "Come on, young'uns, cut that pigeon's wing!" It was the way people shouted for them at cornhuskings, house-raisings—at all the mountain doings.

Nancy looked inquiringly at Grandpa Gruber. He nodded, smiling and clapping. The President was clapping, too. It was all right—it was wonderful!

The judges sat down again as Nancy flung into the old-time clogging dance with Jodey. The buck-and-wing, liveliest of them all! If she'd studied about it a month she couldn't have chosen a better one. Her feet tapped like lightning, heel and toe, heel and toe. Her pink skirt swung out and her yellow hair flung with it.

The boogiewoogie band struck up and swung in with Uncle Badger's banjo. Now they were playing mountain music, the kind that was in their blood. No lagging now, one behind another. They knew what they were playing. And Nancy and Jodey were knocking out the kind of rhythm that had echoed on the cabin floors since the time of Daniel Boone.

"Go it, young'uns!" a shout arose from the crowd. Then people began to sing with the music. They sang till the echoes came back from the face of the big dam towering above them.

> As I was a-wandering down the road
> I met Miss Terrapin and I met Mr. Toad.
> Every time the toad would sing
> The terrapin would cut the pigeon's wing!

Then it was over. The music came to an end. Flushed and smiling Jodey and Nancy stopped dancing. They made their bows and marched from the stage. What a thunder of applause rang in their ears! People clapped and stamped and whistled.

Nancy sat down with her friends, her breath was coming fast and her eyes shining. Had it really happened—had she and Jodey danced at the doin's after all? She could hardly believe it.

"Gollies, Nancy," Dora leaned over to whisper. "You made those jitterbugs look as poor as a cake of soap after a week's washing."

Nancy flashed her a grateful smile.

"If you and Jodey don't get that prize," Bluett exclaimed, "I'll eat my new patent leather shoes!" She held up one foot to show her slipper.

"If you did," Nancy laughed, "you'd feel like coughing them up when you set off home over that rocky path!"

Then a silence fell. The judges had made their decision. One of them was handing a slip of paper up to Grandpa Gruber on the stage. Grandpa took it. He fixed his glasses carefully and read it. Then he looked up and smiled. People grew quiet, holding their breath.

"It looks like the prize for the best dancing goes to the two youngest contestants—" Grandpa paused; then he announced in a loud voice, "Nancy and Jodey Calloway. Come up, young-'uns, and get your reward."

"Hi-yi!" the crowd roared its approval.

In a daze of happiness, Nancy stood up. Jodey joined her. She hardly knew how they got up onto the stage. People were clapping and cheering, even the defeated jitterbugs.

Down the aisle came two young men. Between them they were lugging a heavy package. At their heels two other men were bringing a similar package. The crowd grew quiet, examining those boxes. For weeks they had been trying to figure out the meaning of the verses, trying to guess what these prizes would be. Now they would find out.

"It's not any cherry pie," Jodey whispered. "But it sure is heavy as lead, just as the poem said. Look how those fellows are a-staggering."

The four young men mounted the platform and set the boxes down with a thud, one in front of Nancy, the other at Jodey's feet. "One for each of you," said one of the bearers.

"Open it, open it!" came shouts from the audience.

Jodey and Nancy untied the ribbons and folded back the tissues. A red, shiny object was disclosed in each box. The children stared at the heavy painted things. Were they mechanical churns after all? Nancy thought of the jingle.

It rumbles and it bumbles,
It's stronger than a mule.
It leaves the children time to play
And time to go to school.

No, she couldn't make out what the things were. She looked inquiringly at the young men who had brought them.

They laughed, then one stepped to the front of the stage and recited a jingle.

No more water you need haul.
Press a button on the wall.
This will bring it on the jump—
An electric water pump!

"An electric water pump! Oh, my!" Nancy clasped her hands with delight. Jodey grinned happily. The mountain people broke into waves of cheering and applauding. No more backbreaking work at the old well-curb. No more hauling up bucket after bucket to fill the kitchen barrel. After those electric lines were strung around and those jobs were there for those who wanted them, they'd all have pumps like that!

"Thank you, thank you!" gasped Nancy and Jodey.

Then it was all over and they were on their way home again in the jolt-wagon. Nancy looked at Jodey. "Were you really falling when you tumbled outen that tree or were you just shamming a fall?"

"Shucks, young'un," Uncle Badger put in. "Don't ask questions. It's enough you got to dance. That tumble was opportunity falling right outen the sky. Didn't I tell you it might?"